Kestrel

HANNAH MEREDITH

Singing Spring Press

This is a work of fiction. All names, characters, and incidents are the product of the author's imagination. Any resemblance to actual occurrences or persons, living or dead, is coincidental. Historical events and personages are fictionalized.

KESTREL

Copyright © 2013 by Meredith Simmons

All rights reserved. With the exception of brief quotes used in critical articles or reviews, no part of this book may be reproduced in any form or by any means without written permission of the author.

ISBN: 978-0-9895641-0-6 (Print)
ISBN: 978-0-9895641-1-3 (E-book)

Published by Singing Spring Press

For Mom,

who taught me how to fly

PROLOGUE

Early Spring, 1807

JOSHUA, LORD TRENT, SURREPTITIOUSLY flexed the muscle in his right calf, trying to make a painful cramp go away without alerting Amanda. The position she'd suggested had been exhilarating but damned uncomfortable. He wondered if the author had gotten the description exactly right in the salacious book they'd recently purchased. The human body was designed to bend only certain ways.

Amanda herself was uncharacteristically quiet. Exhaustion or pain? He glanced down at where her head lay on his chest. She seemed comfortably relaxed.

Into the silence, he inserted the topic that had been on his mind since his arrival. "Wish me happy. I'm soon to be wed."

Amanda shot into a seated position as if her entire body had knotted with a cramp. "What? You're getting married!"

She did not sound amused. For some reason, he'd thought she would enjoy the irony of the situation, that they'd have a hearty laugh about his predicament. But Amanda most definitely didn't look like she found anything humorous. Her gorgeous blue eyes had narrowed and she most resembled an angry ginger cat.

"I told you that Uncle Cyril has been pressuring me to find a suitable bride ever since I reached my majority three months ago. Well, he finally came up with what he considers a 'good package,' and so, I am to be wed." As he spoke, Amanda bounced off the bed and began wrapping a sheet around her voluptuous body. "Whatever are you doing?"

"I'm getting dressed," she said, marching away, the end of the sheet trailing after her like the train on a ball gown. "You can hardly expect me to sit around naked while we discuss your upcoming nuptials."

Angry? God, yes. She was spitting mad. Had she thought he would marry *her*? He loved her to distraction, but marriage was impossible. For heaven's sake, Amanda was the widow of a greengrocer. She couldn't even pretend an association with the gentry. And, more importantly, Joshua was supporting her. When it came to marriage, the money needed to flow the other way. That was one thing his uncle had made abundantly clear.

"Amanda, there's no need for you to be upset. My marriage will make no difference to us. As a matter of fact, things will be better. My bride-to-be comes with a very presentable dowry."

He spoke as he, too, scooted off the bed and followed her to the dressing room. En route, he circled back to find his drawers. Amanda was right. This was not a good topic to discuss while naked, particularly when the part of him that she found most appealing did not respond well to arguments and just dangled in a ridiculous manner.

"I'll be able to afford a much nicer house," he said, hopping on one leg as he strove to insert the other in the appropriate opening.

Amanda's head popped around the dressing room door, her brilliant, red-gold hair flaring like a sunburst. "You mean we can lease some place with a better address? I won't have to stay in this pokey old place?"

Joshua pulled his drawers up over his narrow hips. Pokey? He looked around the bedroom. It had cost him nearly a month's allowance to furnish this room alone, not to mention that he'd spent all of his carefully squirreled-away savings on the lease. The address here might not be impressive, but it was certainly respectable and was a cut above Amanda's previous location above the grocery store.

Providing for a mistress had not been easy on the stingy stipend that Uncle Cyril allowed him, but he had scrimped elsewhere to give Amanda what she'd wanted. From the first moment he'd met her, she'd been a fever in his blood. A man had to make sacrifices to get what he really desired.

"Yes, we can find someplace larger and perhaps more modern." He gave her his most charming smile. Joshua had confidence in his charm. It was the one legacy from his father that Uncle Cyril hadn't been able to remove with parsimonious living and constant sermons.

The charm must have worked, since a smiling Amanda came out of the dressing room, the green silk wrapper she now wore displaying her bountiful figure to advantage. When had he gotten her that wrapper? It had been worth whatever he'd paid. The little man in his drawers stirred to life.

"You'll see. This will all be to our good," he said, moving to take her in his arms. She ducked around him, however, and went to sit at her dressing table. Ignoring him, she picked up a silver-backed brush and pulled it through the bright hair he so loved.

"So, who is it that you are to marry?" she asked, looking at him in the mirror.

He felt stupid standing in the middle of the room and went back to lean against the side of the bed. "Miss Clayton, the daughter of the previous Viscount Clayton and the niece of the present one. My uncle seems to think that we will have much in common, having both been raised by our uncles. I guess as a measure of compatibility, this is as good as any."

Amanda held the brush out to him, indicating that she'd like him to brush her hair. "But what is this Miss Clayton like?" she asked as he moved behind her. "You have met her, haven't you?"

"Of course." He watched the silky tresses move through the bristles, releasing a heady, floral scent. "We met last Tuesday when I had my weekly dinner with Uncle Cyril. Viscount Clayton and Lady Clayton were there as well. I evidently passed muster, since after dinner the men met in Uncle's study to go over the marriage settlement—which, I'm sure I've mentioned, was very generous." He tugged gently at her hair and smiled at her in the mirror.

"But what is this bride-to-be *like*? Old? Young? Tall? Short? Does she have a first name?"

Joshua couldn't understand Amanda's interest in a woman who would have no effect on their relationship, but it was obvious that he was going to have to talk about Miss Clayton for whatever reason. He was sure that she had a first name, he must have heard it, but for the life of him, he couldn't remember it. "She's small," he said. "A tiny little thing, like a little brown wren, colorless but apparently cheerful. At least she seemed so when we walked in the garden. And young. She's not yet made her come out. That was evidently planned for this coming Season, but her uncle's new wife is with child, a condition the old goat finds most miraculous, and Clayton feared that seeing his niece through a Season would be too much for his wife."

He put the brush down and dug his fingers into her hair, massaging her scalp. Amanda liked that. "Our marrying without all of the courting ritual seemed a good solution. Uncle Cyril has met with the chit a number of times and finds her amenable." Actually, Uncle Cyril had been effusive about the girl. He seemed to see her as a steadying influence. Cyril's enthusiasm undoubtedly meant that the girl could get a pound's worth of value from a shilling.

"And how long is this betrothal to be?" Amanda pouted so prettily.

"Oh, it will be brief." He stopped rubbing her head and slid his hands along her slender neck, pushing the wrapper off her shoulders, watching the front open to expose the luscious globes of her breasts. "And then we can shop for a new house."

He leaned down to kiss the side of her neck. She arched her back, offering her breasts to his questing hands.

Thank, God. All would be well.

CHAPTER ONE

Fall, 1814

JOSHUA STOPPED HIS HORSE at the top of the rise. His estate, Harkley, spread out before him. This was the scene he'd brought to mind throughout the blood and chaos of war, but in his memory the sun had been shining, making the stones of the house a soft yellow in contrast to the brilliant green of the fields. On a rainy October afternoon, the scene was leached of color and appeared as a study in grays and browns. Joshua shrugged and put the horse into motion. He'd long ago discovered that this was the difference between dreams and reality.

He'd pressed hard to get here. It would be good to be home and out of the damp. Home? He wasn't sure at what point in the past six years Harkley had come to have that designation. For years, the estate had simply been a millstone around his neck, the weight of responsibility that kept him tethered to the ground when he wanted to fly. His change of attitude had probably been aided by others' talk of home. Around countless campfires he'd listened to his friends speak of their homes, the words filled with nostalgia and longing, and his mind had invested this spot with similar emotions.

Home and wife. Once he'd started thinking of Harkley as home, Diana had somehow become part of the equation. Oh, the lies he'd told around those campfires. Had the others embroidered the truth as much as he had? He'd taken the Diana he'd known when they first married and grafted her onto a past that hadn't really existed.

He'd been amazed at how clear his memories of that time were. Diana smiling shyly up at him during their wedding breakfast. The wonder of her hair when he'd released it later that night—a cascade of russet and chocolate that fell nearly to her knees. The overwhelming tenderness he'd felt after they'd lain together, knowing he'd been her first man, her only man. He'd woven these memories into a life that had never happened.

He now accepted the responsibility for having destroyed the possibility of his lies becoming reality. Excuses abounded, of course. He'd been young. Youth tended toward narcissism and melodrama—and he'd felt his great love had betrayed him. But he'd not been that young. No, he'd been more stupid than young. Time had shown that his betrayal of his wife, the little brown wren who'd been placed in his hands for safekeeping, was much worse than anything Amanda had done to him.

It had only taken participation in one battle to change his perspective. He'd escaped unscathed—the fight outside the Portuguese village of Vimeiro had been nearly bloodless compared to what was to come—but there he'd had to shoot his horse, Dancer. Swift and beautiful Dancer, the companion of his youth, his belly sliced by a French bayonet, thrashing in pain until a bullet mercifully ended his suffering. But that shot had also killed his self-absorption. He'd seen the world for what it was and recognized himself as a fool.

And so he'd begun the fiction of a loving wife waiting for him at home. A harmless enough fantasy to keep at bay the horrors that daily surrounded him. Diana had inadvertently supported this illusion with her monthly letters. When one arrived, he would read it privately again and again, as if it were the love note his envious fellow officers imagined. Her notes were brief, a quick recap of estate business such as a land steward might send, but they always ended with *The boy grows apace* or *The boy flourishes* above her signature, *Lady Trent.*

This closure, more than the content, made a lie of his pretense, but the very regularity of the letters' arrivals gave him hope that when he returned, something could be salvaged. If there was one thing Joshua learned from the war, it was that one could live on hope.

The sound of his horse's hoofs on the cobbles of the forecourt brought a boy running from the stable area. Joshua's breath caught in his throat. Had his sins come to greet him before he had even entered the front door? Some unconscious sign to his mount must have signaled danger, since the animal stopped, muscles taut and eyes pricked at the child's approach.

But the boy's face that looked up at him from inside the rain hood was too old, the hair a white blond where he remembered red fuzz. Red fuzz and a miniature hand that had gripped his finger with surprising strength. No, this was not his son.

"If you come to the back door, the cook'll give you food," the boy said. "An' you can sleep in the barn if you like."

"Excuse me?" Joshua asked, confused.

"Our lady aids returning soldiers." The boy gave him a lopsided grin. "Dinnit you see the pot by the gate post? That's the sign you're welcome here."

Joshua hadn't seen the pot since he hadn't been looking for it. All he'd seen was the entry and the lane up the hill to the rise, from which he could see the house. That spot had been his goal. Everything else was peripheral. But the caged hope rose up inside him with the news that returning soldiers were welcome at Harkley. For him, let this be the case.

"I'm Lord Trent," Joshua announced, swinging off the horse and pulling the reins over its head to hand to the boy. "Your lady's husband." The boy's eyes widened and his mouth became a perfect O. "Take the horse to the stables. See him rubbed down good and given some oats."

The boy turned to comply and then swung back around. "What's his name?"

"Not..." Joshua paused. He'd ridden this ugly, Roman-nosed brute for three years and in all that time, had simply referred to him as Not Dead. War was hard on men, but it was hell on horses. No one else had favored the big mouse dun, but he'd proved lucky for Joshua.

"Knot? Like Lover's Knot?" The boy looked hopeful.

"The same," Joshua replied. "But don't use the Lover's part, since it tends to embarrass him."

The crooked grin reappeared, and then the boy led the newly christened Knot away, leaving Joshua standing alone in the rain but feeling better about his homecoming. He mounted the steps and stopped, uncertain, before the door. Should he knock or just walk in? What if he tried the latter and found the door barred against him? He knocked.

Joshua recognized the butler who opened the door. "Putnam," he said. The man was unchanged by the years, still officious looking and portly from good living.

The same could evidently not be said for Joshua, since the butler scowled at him for a full minute before saying, "My Lord Trent. Welcome home." And then he removed his bulk from the opening and ushered Joshua in.

Once in the entry hall, however, they both seemed to have lost the stage directions for this particular play and stood mute and uncertain. Putnam recovered first. "Let me take your coat, my lord. Lady Trent is in the office—but perhaps you'd prefer to freshen up first?"

Joshua divested himself of his sodden greatcoat. The old uniform beneath was equally wet. Yes, he should make himself presentable. Actually, he should have done so before arriving at the door. He sported a two-day stubble and undoubtedly smelled of damp wool and horse. But dashing to Harkley the minute he reached England had seemed important—just as it now seemed necessary to quickly see his wife. She held his judgment in her hands. It was better to know than wonder. "I will see my lady wife," he said.

When Putnam moved as if to guide and announce him, he brushed by the man saying, in a voice now accustomed to command, "I know the way."

If anything in the house had changed, he didn't notice, as he sped like an unerring arrow toward the office. He heard her laughter before he reached the open door. Oddly, he would not have mistaken it for anyone else's laugh. Low and husky for so small a woman, it rang in his memory like a tolling bell.

He stopped abruptly at the door. Diana sat at the desk, illuminated by the glow of a lamp as she leaned forward to examine something on a paper spread across the desk's surface. She was much as he remembered, but the angles of her face seemed sharper. Slight furrows punctuated her brow where before there had been none. An unknown man, sturdy, square-built, his hair slightly frosted with gray, sat across from her. The man who had made her laugh.

Perhaps he made some unconscious sound, for her eyes bounced from the page and locked with his. The same sherry-colored eyes of his dreams, now wide with surprise. A number of emotions flashed there before she schooled her face to blandness. "My Lord Trent. You've returned." She rose to her feet, bringing the unknown man to his as well.

He'd imagined countless versions of this scene. In some, Diana had thrown herself in his arms as she was wont to do in the first months of their marriage. In others, she'd screamed like a fishwife and thrown a costly vase at his head. While this latter behavior was uncharacteristic, it had somehow seemed probable. He'd never envisioned her being polite and distant. And he certainly hadn't expected an audience.

"I came here immediately upon landing. On horseback. My trunk is following." All true, but this somehow seemed irrelevant and stupid. Joshua stepped more fully into the room.

Diana appeared unsurprised by his idiotic utterings. "Oh, I'm sorry, Lord Trent. I don't believe you've met our land steward, George Daniels. Mr. Daniels, my husband, Lord Trent."

Oh, yes, Mr. Daniels. Diana had hired him within a year of Joshua's departure. She'd replaced the former steward for irregularities in the estate books. This information had given him some pleasure, since his Uncle Cyril had hired the previous steward. He'd been gratified to know his omnipotent guardian had been fallible enough to employ someone prone to "irregularities."

Joshua strode forward and shook the man's hand, mumbling the appropriate greetings. Daniels had a strong but not overpowering grip and a pleasant and open countenance. Married with grown children, as

Joshua recalled. He decided to give the man the benefit of the doubt, even if he could make Diana laugh.

"Well, I'm sure you wish to freshen up," Diana said. Odd how everyone kept suggesting this. He must reek of horse. "I look forward to seeing you at dinner. I'm sure you remember we keep country hours."

Then she sat back down and motioned Daniels to do so as well. He'd been dismissed as if he were the lowest subaltern. He was a damned colonel. Twice promoted for merit. Joshua felt his anger rise and then decided this was not the time to take a stand. Diana hadn't launched any pieces of porcelain at his head, so he guessed he should be pleased. He just hoped she hadn't tossed all his old clothes out the window and he had something to wear once he was freshened.

CHAPTER TWO

"No, I don't need a tisane. I don't want anything to drink. My headache will disappear if I just lie down for a while. I'm sure. Please awaken me in time to dress for dinner." Diana felt like she was trying to herd geese without the shooing motion, when with words alone, she finally managed to chase her maid Nan from the room and shut the door in the protesting woman's face. She leaned back against the door and waited to hear Nan leave before turning the key in the lock.

Her eyes swiveled to the door that connected to the master suite. It was locked. Had been for years. But when was the last time she'd checked it? Proud of her restraint, she made herself walk to the wingback chair at the far side of the room and sit down. If she rattled the knob, *he* would know she was just a door away.

Dear Lord, she was becoming ridiculous. She reached up and began removing pins from her hair. Nan must have pulled it up too tightly this morning. Diana felt like she might be getting a real headache instead of a convenient one. The hairpins made little ticking sounds, like restless crickets, as she dropped them on the adjacent table. Yes, her hair had been too tight. Relief came as the heavy, brown waves followed the pull of gravity and dropped down her back and across her breasts.

She leaned back with a sigh and tried to relax. She'd known Trent would soon return. She'd thought she was prepared. His arrival shouldn't have come as a shock. But when she looked up and he was standing there… Something about him had looked wrong. Thinner. Well, thinner was understandable, but at the same time he'd looked bigger, dangerous. Trent was many things, but she'd never considered dangerous to be one of them. His expression had seemed ravaged. She refused to imagine he continued to be devastated by the long-ago departure of his ladybird. Was it so terrible of her to wish for another cause?

Looking back, she realized she'd been pathetically young when she married. She could have refused, she supposed, but once she met Trent, she hadn't wanted to. She thought he was every Christmas gift she'd wanted and not received—all wrapped into one incredibly handsome package. She'd never met, much less conversed with, such a striking and charming man.

He was tall, with pale blond hair and flashing green eyes. His smile, which appeared with regularity, brought forth a dimple on his right cheek. The first time he smiled at her, she'd wanted to hold her finger on that exact spot, waiting for the intriguing indentation to appear. Her urge to touch him had been immediate.

She'd never expected a handsome husband, but she had hoped for nice. When she'd imagined the man she would marry, she had always seen the two of them old, surrounded by children and grandchildren, the unknown man gazing at her with a look of pride. It was probably a vision of her ultimate goal. She hadn't thought she would inspire great love, but was counting on respect and kindness.

It had only taken that one meeting for her to agree with her uncle's choice. She thought she and Lord Trent could have a comfortable life together. She'd been carefully trained to manage an extensive household. She knew how to entertain. She could both competently play the piano and sing. Her needlework was acceptable, and a few of her watercolors were actually quite pleasing.

She'd been a student to make a teacher proud. Her governess had stressed that young ladies who were less attractive should be more competent—and Diana was very competent. Somewhere at the back of her heart lurked the wish that the charming Lord Trent would come to care for his competent wife.

Their wedding ceremony had been small and quickly accomplished with a special license. Diana hadn't minded. She couldn't imagine a large gathering. She'd never been to London. She'd never had a Season. She really knew no one. She'd been raised by her uncle, a kind man, who had been first absorbed by a sick wife and then fascinated by a younger one. Her life on his estate had been lonely.

Then, with a surprising suddenness, she had both a husband and an estate of her very own.

Diana had quickly fallen in love with Harkley. She loved the gracious rooms and the old-fashioned furnishings. She loved looking out her bedroom window at the green fields sprinkled with fluffy white sheep. She'd especially loved the connecting door to the lord's bedchamber that brought her Trent.

She had never imagined that marriage would be like this, a mixture of excitement and contentedness.

She felt she'd been born to be a wife, or, more specifically, Trent's wife.

Even at seventeen, she'd known her own strengths and weaknesses. Her entire life, she'd been told she was unremarkable—brown hair, brown eyes, and a small, sturdy stature—but after her marriage, there was a sparkle about her that made her look almost pretty.

Trent had certainly seemed to find her person acceptable. He visited her every night he was in residence, knocking softly on the connecting door, smiling his devilish smile, asking if she were interested in pursuing an heir.

How she'd enjoyed that pursuit of an heir! In retrospect, her earlier delight in her husband's touch was embarrassing. Trent was often absent, but when he came to Harkley, he was hers. The soft knock, the charming smile, Trent's long, hard body covering hers.

Had there ever been such a deluded idiot?

She'd discovered she was living in a fool's paradise a month into their marriage. Trent had sent a curt message to meet him in the office. She'd arrived to discover her charming husband completely without charm. That meeting remained so clearly in her mind that it might have occurred today instead of nearly seven years ago.

"What do you know about this?" Trent asked, waving some papers clutched in his hand.

"What is it?" Her governess had warned her of husbands' anger over big expenditures, but she had purchased nothing.

"It's our bloody marriage settlement." He thrust the pages at her. *"It's the document that allows my Uncle Cyril, and later, you—my wife, for God's sake—to keep me on a short leash."*

Diana was shocked by Trent's language. This raving, angry man had nothing in common with the kind and considerate person she'd come to know. *"I wasn't privy to our settlement,"* she said, her voice quivering.

"You had no idea that our uncles concocted a document that required either my uncle's, or after your majority, your approval, for the withdrawal of any funds that are not being spent directly on Harkley?"

"Of course not! Our uncles came to the agreement. Didn't you sign the settlement?"

"Yes, I signed the bloody thing, but I certainly didn't read all of it. I saw that nice big number that made up your portion and read no more. I never suspected that as your husband, I wouldn't have access to your dowry. When I applied to your banker to withdraw some of the monies, however, I discovered I had not the right. What garbage!" He threw the offending paper back on the desk.

Sometime during Trent's tirade she'd sat down. A good thing, since her legs felt strangely numb. This *upset was about money. Of course Trent would be disturbed that his wife's income was not his own to use. That wasn't how things were traditionally done.*

"There's a simple solution. I'll just sign whatever it is that needs to be signed." Diana wanted to be conciliatory. She hated to see Trent so overset.

"Don't you understand? You can't do anything until you're twenty-one. I certainly don't want to wait four years to purchase..." His voice trailed off.

"Purchase what?"

"A new townhouse." The words seemed to squeeze out of his throat.

"That doesn't seem so extraordinary," Diana said, relaxing. "If it's your uncle who needs to approve, I cannot imagine this would be a problem. I think it would be wonderful to have a townhouse. I've never been to London and have so longed to go. We could have such fun picking one out. But you said a new townhouse. Do we already have one?"

Trent's face took on an odd look, as if he were a small child protesting that he'd not taken the cookies while his mouth was covered with crumbs. "I've had a townhouse for some time," he said, "but it's," he paused, "pokey."

She almost smiled. How typical of his thoughtfulness. Trent didn't want to take her to a house that he considered small and unfashionable. "Then we will have to get a new one. We can ask your uncle immediately."

He settled a hip on the edge of the desk, his posture casual, although Diana could still see his tension. "It is unlikely that my uncle will approve of anything. He delights in keeping me quite poor. Ever since my father died, every penny the estate has made has to be plowed back into it. You need to understand that Uncle Cyril was my mother's brother and he never approved of my father. I believe that 'wastrel' is the kindest thing that Cyril has ever called him.

"Ever since he gained control of me, my uncle has tried to mold me into a boringly responsible, penny-pinching version of himself." He threw his hands into the air.

"But a townhouse for us would hardly be irresponsible," Diana countered.

"Diana," he said with deceptive calm, "when it comes to London, there will be no 'us.' I have business concerns there and do not need the distraction of a wife. At least for the present, you'll stay here at Harkley. You seem to like it here."

"I, I do like it here. But if you go to London on business, how can we be together?"

His tone gentled, as if he were speaking to someone who was not very bright. "We don't need to be together. Not all of the time. People of our class always have separate lives. It's normal. I have town business and you have the country. Eventually, there will be children to occupy your time."

Something that had been blooming within her began to wither. She leaned forward and grasped his arm. She needed to touch him, to make a physical connection. "But if we are not together, how can we make a child?"

"Do not cling, Diana. It's not seemly. I have every intention of getting an heir; we may have already started one. I'll return often enough to make sure that it happens. But staying here makes me restless. I have to get back to town. I'll leave tomorrow morning."

Diana was appalled to discover tears running down her cheeks. This memory should have lost the power to wound, but it obviously still had teeth. This was not the final sundering—that came nearly a year later with Quin's arrival—but it was the beginning of the end. From that point on, she understood that she had accepted a fantasy as reality, but she had soldiered on, believing that the woman she now knew Trent lived with in town would lose her appeal and that he would return to his faithful and competent wife.

All she'd received for her constancy was her husband's bastard son and a maudlin note. Her first impulse had been to send the child elsewhere and burn the note, but then Quin had given her a great, gummy smile, and she recognized him as the child that should have been hers. Without realizing it, she took the baby into her heart, and he still lodged there. She also kept the note, using the over-emotional and self-serving words as a fortress around that same heart, to protect it from all other inroads.

Lord Trent was now home. But Harkley had become her home more than his. She had made it so. He would have to try to find a way to fit in. She would not be changing.

CHAPTER THREE

JOSHUA WALKED DOWN THE HALL, attempting to breathe. His closet had provided a variety of clothes, none of which really fit. The shirts and coats were all too tight and the pants too loose. He thought he was much thinner than he'd been when he initially went to the Peninsula, so the constriction he felt on his upper body came as a surprise.

Putnam had sent one of the footmen, a nice young man by the name of Royce, to act as his valet. Royce had done his absolute best to turn Joshua out in fashionable attire, obviously hoping this temporary assignment might become permanent. But after forcing Joshua's limbs into this damned jacket, Joshua thought his quasi-valet's talents could be more useful in the kitchen, stuffing sausage into casings.

Hovering in the hallway near the dining room, Putnam gave Joshua a look of critical appraisal. "Royce work out, my lord?"

"Yes. Splendid choice, Putnam." Joshua couldn't fault the man because his clothes no longer fit. He suspected everything was woefully out of style, anyway. Hopefully, Royce could do something to make his uniform presentable until his trunk arrived.

"Lady Trent is already seated," Putnam said without censure, angling his head toward the dining room door.

"Thank you." Joshua entered the dining room, resisting the urge to adjust his cuffs, since no adjustment was possible. The area was alight with a fortune in candles. How many times in the past years had Joshua hunkered over a smoking tallow stub, trying to read? Probably one of Diana's brief missives. *The boy flourishes.* They had much to discuss. But it obviously wouldn't be during dinner.

The table had been expanded so it could have easily seated twenty, but only two places had been set. At opposite ends of the long, mahogany expanse. As if to ensure there would be no meaningful conversation, an audience of footmen hugged the walls, ready to serve. Maybe one of them had been assigned to carry dispatches from one end to the other. That tried-and-true military method seemed the only way he and his wife could communicate.

He bowed in her direction and then took his seat. Diana was even difficult to see from his location. A massive epergne filled with colorful leaves and red berries held pride of place in the center of the table. She appeared as a vague shape beyond the foliage.

The meal passed in silence, punctuated by murmurs to the servers and the clink of silver on china. The food was good. Diana obviously employed a competent cook. The wine, too, was an excellent vintage. Joshua was saddened that his first sumptuous meal in years lacked the enjoyment of companionship.

When only the crumbs of a delectable sugar biscuit were left on his plate, Diana stood and spoke for the first time. "I'll leave you to your brandy, then."

Ah, she'd remembered he preferred brandy to port. Joshua hoped this was a good sign. He stood as well. "Do you normally take tea in the drawing room?" he asked.

"No, in my sitting room."

"Good, I'll join you for tea there."

For the first time, the serene expression he'd observed through the central shrubbery altered. "Light the fire in the blue parlor," she quickly said to a footman. "We'll take tea there." Then she swept out of the room before he could approach her.

As Joshua passed the sideboard, he snagged the brandy decanter and a glass. He wasn't really in the mood for tea.

He trailed Diana into the smaller formal room. If her intent had been to continue to be surrounded by servants, she'd accomplished her aim. Maids, footmen, even Putnam had been pulled into arranging for their mistress's change of plans. "I hope you will not be offended if I remove my coat," he said into the hubbub. "My old clothes are quite constricting."

"Of course. You are at home. Be comfortable." Her reply was absent-minded.

It took Putnam's help to divest him of the confining material. If Diana found the contortions necessary to shed his coat amusing, she gave no indication. And so, he found himself in his shirt sleeves, sitting in a chair flanking the newly kindled fire, staring at his wife across an elaborate tea service.

"That will be all," he said to the last remaining footman. The man looked at Diana for her nod before he complied, but he did leave, closing the door behind him. Somewhere in the room, a clock softly ticked, but Joshua didn't look around to find the source of the sound. His eyes were riveted on his wife.

She wore a garnet-colored dress that showed a lusher figure than he remembered. The roundness of her bust line contrasted with the new angularity of her face. Her chin was sharper, her cheek bones more prominent. She'd tamed her hair into a shining mass that coiled both above and behind. She looked at him expectantly, totally relaxed and contained.

Joshua hoped he gave the same impression. At least he could now move and breathe. "I realize I have wronged you in the past," he said without preamble, "but I want to make amends—to make a fresh start."

"You haven't asked about your son," Diana countered.

So much for trying to approach her with an olive branch. His wife's cool façade masked a smoldering anger. "This is the first time we've not had an audience. Perhaps you wish to feed gossip among the staff, but I do not."

The anger burned through her icy demeanor. "That was hardly your concern when you sent your bastard to me. You didn't worry about what the staff would assume then. You didn't think about how lowering the child's arrival would be for me. In your typical feckless manner, you thought only of yourself. That much was evident from your letter. 'My beloved has left me and abandoned our son.'"

The last was said in such an acid tone that Joshua couldn't doubt Diana was quoting directly from that damned, stupid letter. Unfortunately, he had only the vaguest idea of what he'd written. He'd been in shock at the time and had looked at the bottom of too many bottles of brandy for the events of that day to be anything but a blur.

He assumed Diana had read his rambling missive over and over, just as he'd memorized the note that had begun his idiocy. *Majer Cleese has sed he will mary me*, Amanda had written. *I'm gon to Canida to be wid him. Take the boy.*

His first thought was that Amanda couldn't spell. Then he'd wondered who in the hell Major Cleese was and where she could have met him. And then the import of her message crashed down on him—and logical thought disappeared.

From the distance of all these years, Joshua couldn't begin to understand his reaction. Hell, looking back, he couldn't understand how the woman had ever held him in thrall. But she had. He'd been her slave in every way. She'd tearfully told him she was with child shortly after his wedding—and then continued to cry for the next seven months. Weeping women had always reduced Joshua to a mindless idiot. He did everything he could think of to stop the tears.

But after Quinten was born, he'd supposed that Amanda was happy. Quin had stolen his heart and he thought Amanda had felt the same. That she'd blithely left both of them proved otherwise.

He'd descended into a form of madness. There was no other explanation. He'd decided he, too, could be a major, but a heroic one fighting Napoleon, rather than one who hid from the war in the wilds of Canada. Then Amanda would regret her choice. He sold everything he had and bought a commission.

God, he'd been an ass. The question was how to convince Diana that he had changed.

"I admit the affair was ill handled," he said. "But I've changed. I want to make amends. Tell me what I can do to have another chance."

She abruptly stood, all pretense of indifference disappearing. The tea service rattled as she bumped the table in passing and went to stand before the fire, her back to him. "You could begin by acting like you cared about Quin. You dropped him off on my doorstep as if he were a bundle of dirty laundry. You had no idea what I would do with him when he and that slatternly wet nurse arrived."

She swung around to face him, her color high, eyes flashing. "You abandoned Quin as surely as his mother left you. And you never looked back. You never wrote to ask how he was. You just disappeared."

Everything she accused him of was true, at least to some degree. He could not answer her anger when she was simply stating the truth. He held up his hands in surrender. "The only wise thing I did in this sad chapter of my life was to send Quin to you. I knew you would care for him. I trusted you to do what was right. I couldn't write to you. But that didn't mean I was indifferent to either you or the boy. I was ashamed and had no idea what to say. I still don't. But I knew you took Quin in. Uncle Cyril kept me abreast of what was happening here."

She made a noise that might have been a dry laugh or a snort of disdain. "Just as he let me know that you were still alive. If it weren't for Cyril's passing on information, I could only have believed that you were dead somewhere in Spain. I guess I should be happy that you weren't *too ashamed* to write your uncle."

Diana's sarcasm surprised him where her anger had not. He would have sworn that the girl he married was incapable of using sarcasm like a knife. But then, this was not the girl he'd married. This was someone very different, and his actions had helped make her this way.

"All I can say is that I'm sorry—"

"Sorry? Oh, that makes everything much better. If I'd known you were *sorry*, the concrete evidence of your infidelity wouldn't have hurt so much. I was not so naïve that I didn't suspect you were spending your affection elsewhere, but I stupidly thought you were going through a phase, that if I always welcomed you home without recrimination, your behavior would change. And then Quin arrived. Your son. The child that should have been mine. Do you have any idea what that did to me?"

"Uncle Cyril made your position quite clear."

She again made an odd, dismissive sound. She could have no idea how Cyril had verbally flayed him. As his mother's brother, it was easy for his uncle to blame Joshua's behavior on traits inherited from his father. Cyril had done that all Joshua's life. He'd convinced Joshua that he was destined to follow his father's path of irresponsibility, and then had been surprised when Joshua actually did. It had taken years for Joshua to realize he'd made a practice of living down to his uncle's expectations.

"Cyril told me you appealed to him for help and that the two of you concocted a believable story that accounted for Quin's being here. As I understand it, Quin is purportedly the child of distant cousins on my mother's side. When they died, Quin came here."

"Of course I contacted your uncle." Diana sounded as if she thought Joshua was complaining that she'd done so, when her behavior made complete sense. "I didn't even know what last name to give the child. It certainly couldn't be yours, unless you intended to stunt his future with bastardy. So we chose Rivers, since that entire branch of the family was dead and there would be no one to contest this fiction. Cyril managed to have fraudulent papers drawn up, which named you as guardian. We even had him baptized in the local church. We did everything we knew to protect the child, but you can never claim him as your own without destroying all our efforts."

Joshua already knew this. He understood the necessity. But this didn't mean that having to disavow his own child did not hurt. When he'd first received his uncle's letter explaining what had transpired, he felt as if a French bayonet had found its mark and his guts had been ripped out. Even now, he had to stop his hand from rubbing his stomach. The pain still remained.

"In this I will follow your lead," he said. "But I would like to see the boy as soon as possible."

"He's asleep now, in the nursery. You can visit him tomorrow." Diana frowned at him. "And then I expect you to act the doting cousin."

"I've said I will do so."

"Good. Then I will bid you goodnight."

She crossed the room and exited before Joshua could react, leaving him alone with the dying fire and his untouched brandy. He picked up the latter and took a hefty slug. Had the evening gone well? It was difficult to determine. He had a long way to go to forming a rapprochement with his wife, but he hoped he had made a beginning.

For now, he had to be satisfied that he would see his son in the morning. No, not his son. Quin was his second cousin—or was it third? It really made no difference. The boy could never be recognized as his child. He ran a hand along the waistband of his loose trousers. Yes, the pain was still there.

CHAPTER FOUR

Diana got up early, as she usually did. Overseeing an estate did not facilitate sleeping half the day away. In the past, Trent had always kept town hours when he was in residence. Consequently, she hadn't expected to find him already sitting at the table when she entered the dining room. Annoyance prickled along her back like an unreachable itch.

Thoughts of the man had made sleep impossible for hours, her mind kept alert by all the unanswered questions. She'd pondered the possibility that Trent had actually changed. And then considered that if he had changed, how long this transformation would last. In her limited experience, people's basic nature did not vary, at least for long. People always returned to the point fixed by their character.

As night shadows flickered around her room and the bed linens attempted to strangle her, she finally determined that her husband was still not to be trusted. This decision reached, she then worried about the simple fact that he *was* her husband. He could pound on their adjoining door and demand his marital rights whenever he felt like it. And if this happened, what was she to do?

To deny him was to deny herself, for Quin's presence daily reminded her that she wanted children of her own. And there was only one way for this to happen. She would have to invite her husband to her bed.

She would admit, if only to herself, that she had enjoyed the physical act. When she'd first married, she found this part of her life with Trent to be wondrous. From stray comments overheard at various charitable meetings, she would guess that many women did not find this to be the case.

There need not be an emotional investment in what occurred in the bedroom. She understood that. She knew of many women who loathed the father of their children. But even now, she couldn't hate Trent. Hate what he had done—most assuredly. But the man himself? That was impossible.

She saw him as someone lost and stumbling, but never evil. This seemed a foolish illusion for such a large and virile man, but it was how he came to mind. He'd always treated her with an abstract kindness, as if it were his basic nature to be kind, even if he sometimes became too careless to remember to do so. He was charming and she was not immune to him, even as she told herself charm alone was not enough. She looked back on their nights together with a mixture of tenderness and delight. The delight had stayed in her mind for years, awaking her in the middle of the night and filling her with a longing she didn't want to examine.

Her own ambivalence made her uncomfortable. She did not need him sitting at her breakfast table, smiling his appealing smile, his eyes the compelling green of spring grass in the shade. "Good morning," she said with more abruptness than she intended. "What brings you to breakfast so early?"

"Hunger?" he asked with a quizzical lift of his eyebrow.

She would not find him charming, at least not today. "I imagine you'll want to visit Quin this morning."

"Yes, as soon as possible." He laid his napkin next to his plate as if ready to depart immediately.

"You'll have to wait until I eat, and then I'll take you up."

He got up from the table and refilled his cup from the teapot. "You could have been served," she said.

He looked chagrinned. "I should have remembered that. I've just gotten so used to doing for myself. In Spain, even having tea available was special."

"I understood that officers attended balls and lived well." She filled her plate without looking at him, not sure if the idea of his dancing his way through a war made her feel better or worse.

"Perhaps those attached to a headquarters. I was usually in the field, where things were a bit more rustic. But it kept me busy, and I didn't have that much time to think about what a mess I'd made by my leaving. I can't thank you enough for looking out for Quin."

She had nothing to answer to that, so just shrugged and focused on her meal. Trent didn't say anything else. She soon realized she was bolting her food, reacting to her husband's obvious emotions. Although he wasn't moving, he seemed to quiver like a hound straining for the hunt.

Diana put her napkin down and stood, Trent leaping to his feet almost simultaneously. She repressed a smile. "Shall we go up so you can meet Quin?"

"Yes. Thank you."

He followed her closely as they went up the two flights of stairs. Diana couldn't decide how she felt about this meeting. Part of her wanted Quin and Trent to like each other. They were father and son, after all, even if it couldn't be acknowledged. But another part wanted to keep Quin all to herself. She wanted to be the essential person in the boy's life. She was the one who'd been there for him all these years. Trent shouldn't be able to waltz in and take affection that had been hers.

When she walked into the nursery, however, she discovered that Trent had stopped at the threshold, his eyes riveted on the child sitting on the floor. He was breathing hard and wiping his hands on his trousers. Good heavens. He was nervous. This man, who had fought in a war and had witnessed who knew what sort of horrors, was apprehensive about meeting a six-year-old. The realization filled her with sadness.

Quin saw her, leaped to his feet, and dashed to hug her. "Aunt Di, come look. Someone left these terrific soldiers in a box outside the door last night."

She glanced back at the full-sized soldier hovering just beyond the door. She had no doubt who had left the box. Had he worn his uniform this morning so he would match his gift? She assumed he'd again dressed in his regimentals for comfort's sake. Even she could see the coat he wore last night was too tight. But perhaps his choice of clothing had been designed to smooth his way with Quin. If so, she didn't know if she should praise him for his efforts or look on it as manipulation.

The boy noticed Trent for the first time and huddled further into her skirts. He peeked around her skirts to stare at the strange man.

"Quin, this is my husband, Lord Trent. I've told you about him."

Quin nodded, but still looked unsure. Trent slowly came forward, as if he thought sudden movement might spook his son. He then held out his hand. "Quinten, I'm delighted to meet you. Your aunt has told me so much about you."

But she had told Trent nothing. The realization made her feel petty. She'd used the cryptic final sentence of her monthly notes to exacerbate Trent's guilt. By continuing to write him when he never answered, she was trying to prove that she was the bigger person. She now saw that her letters might have shown her in the opposite light. She'd withheld any real information as a form of punishment.

As he'd been trained to do, Quin came forward and shook the extended hand. Diana could see the gesture made the boy feel very grown up. As for the man...his eyes reflected such a wistful longing she had to look away.

"I'm glad you like the soldiers," Trent said. "They were mine as a boy."

"Truly?"

"Yes. If you look at the blue-coated general, you can see where he's missing part of his foot. I had him out scouting in the garden and he got stepped on by a footman." Trent looked over at her and grinned, making his dimple flash. "That was before I realized generals sat in a tent at headquarters and didn't scout."

Quin grabbed Trent's hand and hauled him to where a battle was taking place on the nursery rug. "Tell me if I have the right people doing the right things."

Soon, man and boy were seated side by side on the floor, carefully discussing strategies as if they were involved in planning an actual war. Diana glanced from one intent face to the other, trying to find similarities.

She'd long known that Quin must resemble his mother in coloring. Trent's hair was an ash blond, while Quin's was decidedly red, which seemed to darken slightly as he aged. For this she was thankful, since it looked as if he were going to avoid a carroty orange. She suspected that as an adult, he would be crowned with hair the color of a bright bay horse. With this coloring, she might have expected Trent's arresting green eyes to stare at her from the boy's face, but Quin's eyes were a frosty blue. Again, perhaps the legacy of his mother.

It was impossible to tell at this point if Quin would eventually reach his father's height. Boys grew in such fits and starts. She could see no similarity in their facial features. The softness of youth kept Quin from resembling Trent, although she couldn't imagine the boy would ever develop the stark, vertical cheek bones and blade of a nose that belonged to the man.

What they did have in common was the ability to become absorbed in the imaginary battle taking place. Both of them wore similar looks of concentration. Then Quin suddenly laughed at something Trent had said, and in the quick turn of the head, his hand coming across to brush some errant hairs from his face, she oddly saw herself.

Gracious. She didn't have all day to stand around and watch two boys play with soldiers, for that is what they appeared to be. She had an estate to run and decisions to make.

Without disturbing the two of them, she made her way out of the nursery and into the real world of adults. A pain deep in her chest made her wonder if she was leaving something important behind.

CHAPTER FIVE

JOSHUA TILTED THE GLASS FROM side to side, watching the amber liquor swirl about. The moving brandy picked up pieces of the firelight, making it appear as though he held flames in his hands. He was pleasantly tired, but the day's events circled his mind and kept him from seeking his bed.

My God, Quin was a wonder. The boy was filled with so much love and laughter. Joshua felt an abiding sadness for all the years of his son's life that he'd missed, but he could look forward to the years to come with hope. The toy soldiers had been an excellent way to make a connection. When Joshua had sat in this same chair the night before, worried about meeting his son for the first time, he'd remembered their existence. His fondest memories of his own father involved the times they'd sat on the nursery floor with legions of those same soldiers spread out around them.

His Uncle Cyril had done his best to eliminate Joshua's father's influence, but he'd been unable to smother those early memories. Joshua now hoped that when Quin was approaching thirty, he, too, would have similar memories of his Uncle Josh.

Uncle Josh, the name he would forever be known by. Diana was right. To claim any other relationship could only hurt the boy. But heaven help him, how that fact hurt the man. Joshua realized this was just one of the many accommodations he would have to make to bring his life back to where it always should have been.

Diana was a totally different part of the equation. She was definitely his wife by law and now by his inclination. The difficulty was in getting her to be his wife in actuality. He knew there were some injuries that went so deep they never really healed. He fervently prayed his actions hadn't inflicted such a grievous hurt.

He hoped he was making some headway in proving that he had changed, but couldn't be sure. Diana had been surprised when she'd come into the office this afternoon to discover he'd had a second, smaller desk moved into the room and placed against the wall furthest from the big, master's desk.

She seemed quite shocked that he was sitting at the smaller desk.

"I thought I'd need a desk if I'm to learn how to manage Harkley," he'd said by means of explanation.

"But…" She'd gestured at the larger desk.

"That desk belongs to the person who is running the estate, and right now, that person would be you. I hope the time comes when I'll feel confident to take that place, but I have much to learn. With you and Mr. Daniels acting as my mentors, this should eventually occur. Until that time comes, however, I have no intention of encroaching on your position."

Was it possible for a woman to grow as one watched? Joshua could have sworn that happened. Diana had always been diminutive, but she suddenly seemed to increase in stature. Then she'd gone to her desk, extracted the last quarter's books, and brought them to him, standing close as she pointed out various entries. Her skirts brushed his legs and her subtle fragrance filled the air around him. It was wonderful.

She'd finally settled at the larger desk, and they sat in companionable silence as each did his own work. Joshua had always hated the bookkeeping part of estate management, yet for the two hours they were both in the office, he couldn't imagine anywhere else he would want to be.

Thinking back on the peaceful time he'd enjoyed this afternoon, Joshua chuckled and took a sip of brandy. Sometimes his change of attitude even surprised himself. He suspected he would be unrecognizable to some of the friends he'd had before he left for the military. He wondered if they would now like him—and more importantly, if he would like them.

The sound of a key turning in a lock brought his head up from his contemplation of the fire. A key in a lock. His comfortable lethargy slipped away to form a battlefield alertness. The only locked door was the one that connected to Diana's rooms. He knew it was secured against his opening it. He'd tried it the first time Diana had definitely been in another part of the house.

But now, the door he'd thought immovable slowly swung in and Diana appeared. The hand holding the glass tightened to the point of pain and his breath caught in his throat. She wore a peach-colored dressing gown and stood bathed in candlelight, her dark hair loose and curling around her body like a thing alive. She was the dream he'd conjured on so many dark nights while he'd stroked himself to completion.

Fear suddenly banished lust. "Is Quin all right?" he asked, standing to face her.

"Yes. Forgive me. I didn't mean to startle you. I only..."

Only what? his mind screamed, but he remained silent, afraid he would say something wrong and she would disappear back into her rooms, perhaps never to return.

"I, eh, only wanted to talk to you." She seemed nervous, skittish.

"Please come in and sit down." He motioned to an adjacent chair. "I was enjoying a nightcap. Would you like one?"

"No. No, thank you. I seldom drink spirits this late."

She sat down and he followed her lead. Small talk evidently having run its course, they sat looking at one another in silence. There was nothing companionable about this lack of sound, however. It scraped across his skin, drawing a slight tremor and gooseflesh in its wake.

"I think I actually would like a brandy," she suddenly said.

Joshua leaped from his seat as if prodded by a burr. His hand trembled on the decanter and he had to hold it well above the glass to avoid ticking on the rim. God, he should not be so undone, but she had caught him unprepared. With effort, he mastered himself and took her the drink.

"Thank you. I'm sorry. I feel terribly awkward." She gave him a shy, uncertain smile, very like the ones she'd gifted him with when they were first married. "I wanted to say how pleased I am that you and Quin got along so well today. He was over the moon that you've offered to give him riding lessons.

I'm afraid I've been remiss in that department, since I don't ride myself."

"You've been remiss in nothing. You've done a wonderful job with him. Quin is a delightful boy. Bright, happy, sturdy. Heavens, when I picked him up I couldn't believe how heavy he was." He realized his mouth had turned up in his charming smile, but it had been uncalculated, real.

It quickly fell away when he saw her looking down, watching her hands make pleats on the lap of her robe. Perhaps he shouldn't have picked the child up. Had he inadvertently trespassed into an area that belonged to Diana?

She looked up and gave him another slight smile. "Having you here will make a big difference to Quin—and all for the good. I can see where he could use a man's influence."

"You know I'll never do anything with him that you don't approve of. And if I ever should, please tell me immediately and I'll desist. In no way do I want to usurp your authority."

"I trust that we both have his best interests at heart," she said, settling back in the chair, pulling the dressing gown taut over her breasts and opening the neckline to show a white nightgown beneath. How had he never realized that she was beautiful? But then, he'd been an ass, obsessed with a flamboyant woman who had made him feel like a man when he was far from acting like one.

Oddly, he could now think of Amanda without rancor. Time and, hopefully, maturity had given him the perspective to see she'd thought he was a way to escape a humdrum widowhood. In return for a perceived better life, she'd given him the illusion of love. What a disappointment he must have been, satisfied to always keep her in the shadows and marry another.

What he'd viewed as the worst sort of betrayal had evolved into an understanding that Amanda had done the pragmatic thing. Her Major Cleese had offered her marriage, a secure future not tied to the whim of a boy pretending to be a man. Of course she had followed him to Canada.

And the kindest thing she'd done, he now saw, was to leave Quin with him. "Yes, we both want only the best for him," he said sincerely.

Diana took a large swallow of the brandy, as if fortifying herself. "Quin, of course, cannot inherit. It was this fact that left me in such an untenable position while you were gone. If something had happened to you, I would have been left with nothing."

"That is not true." Joshua felt a need to defend himself. "My uncle sent assorted legal documents chasing after me all over the continent. I know I signed one that assured the return of all your dowered funds, as well as a widow's stipend from the estate, if I'd fallen in battle. You would hardly have been left penniless."

"That's true. But Harkley would have gone to some distant cousin. Doesn't it bother you that you would have lost your patrimony to a virtual stranger?"

At the time he'd fled his supposedly great, and decidedly childish, disappointment, the disposition of Harkley had been the farthest thing from his mind. It was only later that he'd come to appreciate the estate, to long for a continued connection to his father's family. For a while, he wondered if his initial disinterest was the product of Cyril's constant disparagement of the Trent side of his heritage. He'd eventually come to understand that his uncle was angry at the way Joshua's father had treated his mother, Cyril's sister. In and of itself, there was nothing wrong with being a Trent. Particularly if he stopped behaving like one.

Joshua tempered his annoyance. "I know Harkley has come to mean a great deal to you. Anyone can see that from the care you've taken with the estate. I'm sorry you feared for its loss."

"I'm still unprotected if anything untoward should happen to you," she stated baldly. Her hands, which continued to fold patterns into her robe, were the only indication that she was not completely calm. "My only protection would be to have your son."

She brought her eyes up to look into his. Beautiful eyes, the color of morning tea in a fine china cup. Tendrils of hope tightened around his heart. Was she suggesting what he thought she was? "Would you like us to try to make a child?" he asked in a voice suddenly hoarse.

"Yes. I mean, you once wanted an heir, and I thought..."

She'd gone back to watching her fingers crease the material on her lap, but Joshua well remembered their laughing heir hunt. He would enter her room at night and ask if she wanted to go in pursuit of an heir. And those nights had been sweet. The distance of time had made him realize he'd been doing more than just his duty. He was sure Diana had been more than dutiful—and perhaps she could be again.

"Yes, I'd very much like an heir. But more importantly, I'd like to get that heir with you, Diana." He wondered if it was the harsh pounding of his pulse that made his voice quiver. He so wanted to do this right. He *needed* to do this right. All of his fantasies seemed possible. But, dear Lord, he had to do this right.

He realized with shock that he'd never really seduced anyone. He'd just turned on the fatal Trent charm and it had happened. But now, when he needed it more than breath, that charm seemed to have deserted him. He was left with only himself,

Joshua, wanting this to work more than he'd ever wanted anything.

He stood slowly. He didn't want to frighten his amazing, little brown wren. He covered the distance between their two chairs in just a few steps. He extended his hand. "Would you like to begin the pursuit of an heir tonight?"

Say yes. Say yes. The words echoed through him, but he didn't give them voice.

He was sure he'd stood with his hand extended for an eternity when she finally looked up at him. She simply nodded, slipped her hand into his, and rose. Together, they moved toward his bed. Somewhere an orchestra played, the music rising to a crescendo. Joshua was positive he heard it.

CHAPTER SIX

IT WAS SO SIMPLE—and impossibly difficult. Trent's broad hand filled her vision, the firelight picking out calluses that hadn't existed in the past. Diana raised her face to look directly into his. The deep green of his eyes was unchanged, but now the corners showed a web of fine lines. *Yes*, she screamed in her head, but the word couldn't get past her frozen lips. All she could do was slip her hand into his and stand. But that seemed to be enough.

He led her toward the big tester bed, a bed she'd never visited. Trent had always come to her. The covers had been turned back by a servant and the bed should have looked inviting. Instead, it seemed too high, too wide, too foreign. The dark blue hangings put the entire area into deep shadow. Her feet slowed.

When Trent turned with a quizzical look, she said, "Maybe we should go to my room."

He shifted toward her in what she thought was compliance, but as she moved in the direction of the connecting door, he stopped her with a hand on her shoulder.

"Why?" He uttered the single word with the softness of a sigh.

"We always were in my room before..." How did she explain she was nervous and needed the familiar? As much as she wanted her own child, the process of getting one suddenly seemed like too much of a commitment. She didn't think she would be able to remain indifferent to this man—and indifference was the emotion she needed to nourish. Already, heat spiraled up her arm from where he held her hand. His touch on her shoulder was beginning to warm. She realized that by accident or design, they had touched very little since his arrival. Her brain didn't function properly when they had physical contact.

"I'd really like us to stay here," he said. "I don't want things to be like they were. Leave the past in the past. I want to start something new, better."

He released her shoulder and ran the back of his fingers along her jaw line. She wanted to press back into his hand, like a cat begging for a treat. At that lowering thought, her body stiffened. She was not some hungry animal thankful for the least attention.

Trent must have felt her rigidity. His hand dropped from her face. "We don't have to do this if you don't want to. But I'm willing to admit that I want this very much. Have wanted it for years. I long for a connection, an end to loneliness. I've dreamed of home, of family, and you've been at the center of this dream. Let us make a new beginning. Let us see what we can build together."

His tone was filled with a wistful yearning that vibrated through her like a tuning fork set to the same note. Was a new beginning possible? And was she willing to wager her heart on this possibility? He'd hurt her more deeply than she liked to admit. She didn't want to open herself to such agony again, but to *not* take the chance was to guarantee that her own emotional isolation would continue, perhaps forever.

"I'd like to try, Trent."

He chuckled softly, and his hand returned to push back her hair and softly trace the arch of her brow. "Well, a good beginning would be for you to call me Joshua."

"But you told me to call you Trent, that your family always called you by that name." She distinctly remembered the conversation, which had taken place a few days before their wedding. She could now see that having to ask him what she should call him indicated how little they'd known each other at the time.

"My only family is Uncle Cyril, and he does call me Trent, but I told you to do so to keep you at a distance. It was a foolish request and one of the many things I've come to regret. I really would like you to call me by my given name."

"Joshua," she said, the name surprisingly comfortable on her tongue, as if she'd always thought of him as such. She leaned into his stroking hand, which he slipped back to cradle her head as his face lowered toward hers. His mouth brushed hers lightly, like the touch of a butterfly. It was oh, so sweet.

She strained upward, trying to increase the pressure of his lips. Instead, he wrapped his arms around her, pulling her flush with his body. Her face nestled into his chest, his old uniform shirt still retaining a faint smell of horse and warm male. He kissed her softly on top of her head and then swept her up into his arms. In a few quick strides, he deposited her on the bed, legs dangling over the side.

"Now those tempting lips are easier to reach," he said, bending to capture her mouth. He traced her lips from one side to the other as if learning a new terrain. Heat flowed through her and her hands came up to encircle his neck. She opened her mouth slightly and welcomed the play of his tongue. Dear Lord, she'd missed this.

He pulled back from her, his face intent as he untied the sash of her dressing gown and slipped it off her shoulders. To facilitate its removal, she lowered her arms, then grasped him around the waist once her arms were freed. His mouth returned to hers, hot and hungry, sweetness only a memory.

She responded in kind, leaning forward to rub her aching breasts against his chest. His hands roamed her body, teasing her nipples and molding her hips. Her breath came in pants and dampness pooled between her thighs. She wanted him over her, in her. She wanted him, Joshua. She wanted—everything.

He pressed her back onto the bed, his body settling comfortably between her legs. Supporting himself above her, he traced his lips down her neck and across her collarbone. Roving lower, he licked one tightly furled nipple and then the other, finally suckling each through the thin material of her nightgown.

Diana made odd, mewing sounds. Her fingers tangled in his hair and she wantonly arched up toward him. She wanted more contact. "Naked," she said, shocked that the errant thought had been vocalized.

Joshua heard it, however, and raised his head. "Excellent suggestion," he said, a wicked smile flickering across his face, calling the dimple out of hiding. He picked her up and laid her more fully on the bed, her head on the pillow. Simultaneously, one hand gathered the hem of her gown. He laughingly pulled it up until the material pooled about her head, obscuring her vision. She raised her arms and Joshua whisked the gown away, allowing her to see again.

He hovered above her, all humor gone. He shifted away, a look of intense concentration on his face. She felt embarrassed, lying naked under his perusal. Perhaps she unconsciously flinched, as if to cover herself, for his hand shot forward and touched her torso.

"I imagined you like this so many times, but my memory didn't do you justice." His voice was low, husky. "So damned beautiful." His fingers began to trace up and down her body, leaving fire in their wake. His eyes followed the progress of his hand with complete absorption.

And for at least this brief span of time, Diana felt beautiful. No longer just competent and cheerful, but alluring. "I imagined this, too," she said, "but you were wearing fewer clothes."

Her words seemed to break a spell and Joshua's smile returned. "As my lady commands."

He slipped from the bed, already pulling his shirt over his head. The firelight cast his defined musculature into bold relief. This was not the body she remembered. His shoulders were broader, upper arms heavier. Muscles crossed his abdomen in ripples. Everything about him was solid, hard, where she recalled some softness. The years had burned that away and left only the essential man. He turned away from her and shucked his pants and small clothes together, bringing his buttocks and sculpted thighs into prominence.

Then he faced her and she caught her breath. With his blond hair and arresting face, she had always thought he looked angelic, but now, Michael, the warrior archangel, stood before her. She noticed the fine line of a scar running diagonally across his chest and a round, puckered scar riding on his left side below the waistline. But what was most noticeable was the jut of his arousal, rising from a thatch only slightly darker than his hair.

He smiled as if he knew of her appraisal. Then, with unhurried motion, he returned to her, stretching his long length along her side, again sweeping a warm hand over her body. His mouth came down on hers, claiming her. His hand stroked the juncture of her thighs, his fingers moving into the seam there, bringing her hips up off the bed in an involuntary response. Those clever fingers moved in and out in the same rhythm he tongued her mouth.

She was not quiescent. Her hands drifted over his body, learning it as though blind. The springy softness of the hair on his chest. The oddly wrinkled texture of the scar on his side. The power of muscles that flexed under her touch.

They were both gasping for breath and sweat sheened when he finally came over her. He positioned himself between her legs, elevated her hips, and entered with one sharp stroke. She'd forgotten the wonder of his filling her. And then he began to thrust and she was lost. No thought was possible, only sensation.

She spiraled higher and higher. The force of her desire rose up under her like the wind beneath the wings of a hawk, and she went up and up, glorying in the freedom. Until she reached the pinnacle and fell, swooping greedily for the prize.

As if her completion called to his, Joshua stiffened, crying out her name. He gathered her to him and rolled so she now lay across him, her head resting on his chest. She lay there replete, listening to the rhythm of his heart return to a slower beat.

He softly rubbed his hand up and down her back. When the motion stilled, she looked up to see that he slept. His long, pale lashes fell on a face that would never again be boyishly handsome. But the new version was even more compelling.

She loved him. Probably always had. And she didn't *want* to. He'd already demonstrated that loving him led to heartbreak, but she couldn't help herself. He was the love of her youth, and while he'd proved to be flawed, she couldn't change her emotions. But she certainly didn't want Joshua to know how she felt. Only a fool would display such vulnerability when he would never love her in return.

She wondered if he were even capable of love. Obsession, definitely, since he'd demonstrated that with his mistress. But she doubted what he'd felt for this other woman was actually love. Had that been the case, he would have damned convention and married her.

But the counterfeit of love that she'd just experienced was very, very good. Well, perhaps "good" was too weak a word. She felt a flush of embarrassment when she remembered how she had shortened his name to Josh and had called it out, over and over again, in time to his thrusts.

A lifetime of such nights was something to look forward to. If she could just keep Joshua's interest enough for him to remain at Harkley, they could build a life. Her ever-hopeful heart placed an aged version of his face on the man in her original imagining of her married life. They would be surrounded by children and grandchildren, and he would look at her with pride. And that would be enough. It had to be.

The chill of the room was becoming uncomfortable, so she reached down and drew the covers over both of them. When Joshua had visited her, he'd always returned to his own room. She wanted to break that pattern. Lying here with her head resting in the hollow of his shoulder was too appealing to forsake. She felt all her muscles relax as she melted into his warm body, and the solid beat of his heart lulled her to sleep.

CHAPTER SEVEN

Winter, 1814

THE COLD HAD LONG AGO seeped through the layers of clothes that wrapped his body, and his gloved hands felt numb and unresponsive, but Joshua was warmed by a feeling of accomplishment. It was, nonetheless, good to be home. He brought Not to a stop at the stable door, and Toby, the boy who had initially greeted him, came scuttling out into the blustery day.

"Oh, good, you got her," the boy said, taking the lead rope Joshua extended and guiding the pretty bay pony into the open stable door.

Joshua swung stiffly from the saddle and followed Toby into the relative warmth of the barn. "Mr. Daniels was right to suggest Hargrove's farm, and this mare in particular. She has both a lovely temperament and a smooth gait. Do you think Quin will like her?"

"He'd have to be crazy not to," Toby said, envy plain on his face.

Joshua had been giving Quin riding lessons on an old carriage horse, the Harkley stables containing no other animal remotely suitable for a novice six-year-old. While docile, the horse was hard-mouthed and stubborn and placed Quin entirely too far from the ground for Diana's comfort. It was obvious a different mount was needed. His search for just the right pony had taken him longer than he'd anticipated, but he was confident that he'd found the right animal.

"What's her name?" the boy asked.

"Caprice."

Joshua saw Toby mouth the name and frown. "I'll call her Cappy then."

"Good choice." Joshua busied himself with removing Not's tack, wondering how a plain brute like Not had ended up being called Lover's Knot and a graceful beauty like Caprice was christened Cappy. Life was filled with inconsistencies that made no sense.

"Excuse me," said an unknown voice. "Is this estate Harkley?"

The open barn door framed a mounted man. A soldier, by the look of him, although his uniform was hidden by his greatcoat and scarf. Joshua assumed he was one of the returning soldiers who found their way to the house because of the pot by the gatepost. Joshua had been surprised at how often these men arrived, always in need of food and shelter. England would soon be awash with ex-military men. But most new arrivals had no idea of the name of the estate.

"You're correct," he said. "This is Harkley and I'm the owner, Lord Trent. How may I help you?"

The man dismounted and moved forward. In the gray light of a winter's afternoon, he looked totally average, with a square face and light brown hair. "I'm Major Harold Cleese."

Joshua stilled. Major Cleese? Could this be Amanda's Major Cleese? He looked behind the man to see if a woman accompanied him, but there was no one else. Thank the Lord. He and Diana had been getting along so well—she was almost nightly in his bed, a wonder he didn't want to disturb—and the arrival of his former mistress would definitely have led to a disturbance.

"What may I do for you, Major?" Joshua asked, but he didn't move forward to greet the other man. If this were indeed Amanda's major, there was no need to pretend friendship. Any anger he'd felt had long since burned away, but Joshua still had no desire to know the man.

"I'm looking for my son."

Relief nearly folded Joshua's stiffened legs. Thank God—this wasn't Amanda's major. This man's appearance was nothing more than another example of life's inconsistencies. Two men with the same name were not that much different from two names for the same horse. There would be no assault on his relationship with his wife from this direction, but the man's request confused him. "Your son? I'm afraid you have me at a disadvantage. I don't know who you're talking about. But if you've lost a child, I'll be happy to turn out my staff to help find him. No boy should be wandering around on a day this inclement."

The soldier's face hardened into stubbornness. "Don't play dumb with me, Trent. My son. The kid Amanda fobbed off on you. I want him back. Is this the boy?" The man nodded at Toby, who stood silently currying the new pony and absorbing every word that was being said.

Realization knifed through Joshua, making him colder than any winter weather ever could. This was indeed the man who had married his former mistress, and the child he was asking about could only be Quin. Quin, whose position in life could be threatened by anything that was about to be disclosed.

"Toby, go up to the house and ask Cook to make a food packet for this soldier. Stay there. He'll pick it up when he leaves."

"But, milord, I ain't finished with the mare." Like most boys his age, Toby knew when he was being asked to miss something intriguing.

"I'll take care of her. Now get on up to the house."

Toby laid the currycomb on the wall of a stall and reluctantly left. Major Cleese's eyes followed his every move.

"If that's my kid, sending him up to the house won't do any good. I've got a letter signed by Amanda attesting to my paternity. I was her husband. Any court in the land will see the boy returned to me, even if I'm not some high and mighty lord."

Joshua focused on Cleese's use of the past tense in referring to Amanda. The rest of his assertions were too terrible to consider. "Where is Amanda?"

"Dead. Two years ago. She died having my babe while I was freezing my arse off chasing those damned Americans around Canada. Unlike all these supposed heroes returning from the continent, those of us who fought in Canada had to battle the elements as well as the enemy. When I got back to where I was billeted, she and the babe were already buried. But she left me a letter where she begged my forgiveness for leaving my son with you so she could more easily get to Canada. So, while I appreciate you taking care of him, now that I'm in England, I want him back."

Cleese had walked into the stable as he spoke. From closer examination, Joshua could see the major was significantly older than he was. His brown hair was heavily streaked with gray and his weathered face cut deeply with wrinkles. He was, nonetheless, a compact and powerfully built man who moved with a vigorous step.

Joshua had no doubt, however, that he could take the man down. His fists clenched and his muscles tightened. He would shut the delusional bastard's mouth, one way or another.

"You have no son here," he said. "Before she married you, your wife bore me a child who was the result of an illicit liaison. In short, Amada was my mistress. That, I'll admit. But you must already know this. I have no idea how you arrived at your fantastical conclusion, but at the time *my* son was conceived, you were nowhere around."

Cleese laughed, an ugly sound filled with derision. "Which shows how little you understood what was going on. I knew Amanda long before you arrived on the scene. I honorably courted her, wanted to marry her, but then you showed up. Lord Trent, hanging about with puppy devotion. She was thrilled a lord was interested in her and couldn't see any value in a major who had worked his way through the ranks. My God, man, she saw you as her chance for betterment. She imagined you'd marry her. She spent hours writing the name Lady Trent over and over in a little book she kept in her secretary drawer.

"But I knew her pathetic dreams would never come true. I told her she was nothing to you but a quick tup. You'd never consider marrying someone of her class. I visited her whenever you were off doing your noble duties, cozying up to your uncle or courting the nonentity with a full purse that you married. After your fumbling around in the dark, she needed a real man to remind her what loving was all about."

"She lied to you," Joshua said, wishing he were more confident of his position. Had Amanda entertained this man when Joshua wasn't around? The idea rankled, especially since he was paying for everything. But he would have known. Surely, he would have known. *Fumbling around in the dark* was definitely a lie. He knew when a woman was satisfied. And damn her eyes, Amanda had been well satisfied. If one part of her supposed letter was false, then the whole probably was. "She lied," he repeated.

"She didn't!" Cleese's voice rose to a shout. "She left me a letter. She knew whose son the child was. I think she hoped to use the kid as leverage to get you to the altar, but by the time she was sure she was breeding, you'd already married your money bags. I'd been posted to Canada by then, but I sent her money to come to me, and she did. In her letter, she told me she felt guilty about leaving the boy, since he was mine. And if you don't hand him over, I'll raise hell through the courts—and I'll win. Courts pay attention to dying declarations."

"I very much doubt the courts will ever hear such a case." Diana's clear voice echoed through the barn with surprising strength. Joshua's eyes jerked in the direction of the sound and saw her standing at the door. He was shocked to see that she held a pistol gripped in both her hands, a pistol pointed unerringly at Major Cleese. "The boy you seek is not here. So it would be a good idea for you to get back on your horse and leave. If this doesn't happen, the magistrate will hear a tale about how one of the returning soldiers the estate tries to help attacked me and I was forced to kill him in self-defense. I guarantee that every person on Harkley will testify that this is exactly what transpired."

"Diana, what in the bloody hell are you doing here?" The words leaped from his mouth before his brain was functioning. He immediately regretted them when she slid him a dismissive look.

"I'm here because Toby came running to the house, saying there was a strange man here who was a threat. Did you really think he wouldn't stay and listen?"

She raked both of them with a glare made more disturbing because he'd never seen such an expression cross her face. "I guess I could stand here all afternoon and wait while you both whipped out your cocks to decide whose was bigger, but that seems like a waste of time. I simply want this lunatic who imagines anyone at Harkley is related to him to leave." She looked directly at Cleese, on whom the gun had unwaveringly been trained. "Or I *will* shoot you."

With blinding certainty, Joshua had no doubt that Diana would follow through with her threat. He hoped that Major Cleese could also read the seriousness of her intentions. Joshua didn't recognize this woman, but Lord, she was magnificent. Had the Diana he thought he knew ever existed, or was he as deluded as Major Cleese?

She raised the pistol and confidently sighted down the barrel. "You really should leave, now."

CHAPTER EIGHT

THE MUSCLES ALONG THE tops of Diana's arms burned with the effort to hold the gun steady. When she'd shot at targets, she hadn't maintained a shooting stance for this length of time. But she would keep the gun trained on the man who'd come to claim Quin until either he left or she shot him. The longer he tarried, however, the less she was concerned about which outcome occurred.

Toby's account had been garbled, all rushed words and waving hands. But she'd understood enough to immediately retrieve the dueling pistol from her desk drawer and load it. She'd arrived in time to hear the man's audacious claims. What he threatened wouldn't come to pass, however. She would see to that.

The interloper stared at her and then foolishly dismissed her. His reaction was plainly written on his face. He turned back to look at Joshua, as if her presence meant nothing. "This is what you chose over Amanda? You must have needed her money more than I thought."

Did he think to wound her with his words? She'd always known where her value lay, and if there had been any doubt, Quin's arrival and Joshua's departure had made that clear. But over the years, during which she'd had complete control over Harkley, she'd come to realize she was so much more than the woman who brought needed money to the estate. Her insights and wise leadership were appreciated by everyone in the district. She herself was worth more than any funds that came with her. She was even beginning to think that Joshua realized her value.

Before Joshua could speak and perhaps disabuse her of this growing confidence in his feelings for her, she said, "The boy you seek isn't here. Has never been here. We are guardians of a distant cousin's child. We have all the legal documents to prove this is the case. His name is Quinten Rivers. He was baptized at the village church. He's our ward and no relation of yours. And if you say otherwise, you'll be the one in court, charged with malicious slander."

The man glared at her with anger. "If you think I'm going to be taken in by a fantasy concocted by some hoity-toity bitch—"

While the stranger's attention was fixed on her, Joshua covered the distance between them and doubled the man over with a blow to his midsection. The man straightened and swung wildly at Joshua. Ducking the punch, Joshua delivered his own to the man's unprotected chin. His legs folded and he hit the ground. The stranger tried to rise, but fell back with a groan.

Joshua went to stand over the prone man. "Get on your feet and get out of here before either I beat the hell out of you or I get out of the way so my wife can shoot you." His voice was a growl punctuated by heavy breathing.

Diana felt a spurt of irritation. The stupid man looked more frightened by Joshua's fists than he'd been by her gun. She tried to convince herself that she should be satisfied he was at least afraid. Despite his attitude, she kept her pistol pointed at his chest as he awkwardly got to his feet, hands extended from his sides in a show of compliance.

With careful slowness, he reached up to wipe the blood that trickled from his mouth. He looked between Diana and Joshua and shook his head. "I can't figure out why your wife would want to keep the little bastard, even if he were your get."

"Because *here* he isn't a bastard," Diana said, conviction ringing in her voice. "And I really don't care which of you fathered him. Neither of you has been anywhere around for his entire short life. But I have. I'm the one who chased away nightmares. I'm the one who helped him walk, who laughed when he fell. I'm the parent here. One of you just filled the role of stud, nothing more."

Surprisingly, Joshua smiled at her insult. "I think you have the right of it. And since I'm the resident stud, Major Cleese will be leaving." Without taking his eyes off the man, Joshua came to her and gently removed the pistol from her hand, casually pointing it at the other man.

Bereft of the gun's weight, her hand began to tremble. She jammed her fists into her skirts, where the tremors would be less noticeable. She straightened her spine and frowned at the intruder.

Using the pistol to point the way, Joshua motioned toward the man's horse, which was still standing in the open door. "Off with you, then. There's nothing here for you."

The stranger scowled but complied. He mounted and slowly walked his horse down the lane. Joshua came over to her, opened his greatcoat, and folded her into his arms, wrapping the coat around her. His warmth enveloped her. Shivering, she leaned into his body, realizing she was frozen to the bone. He dropped his chin onto the top of her head. They held that position as the soldier slowly faded from sight in the late afternoon gloom.

"Do you think he'll be back?"

She felt his shrug through her back. "There's no way to tell, but we'll alert everyone on the estate to keep a watch for him. If he does return, I'll go to the magistrate and have him hounded out of the county."

"But then the truth of Quin's background will come out." She began to tremble, horrified that her eyes were filling with tears. She abhorred weakness, and her behavior was weak. But her fear was for Quin. She would hate to see his life stunted in any way.

"There's no chance that will happen. You've already explained to the major how such a disclosure would turn out. You, my brilliant wife, set up a background for Quin that will hold up to any scrutiny. If Cleese insists on making everything public, there are a few who will believe him, but more will believe he has some ulterior motive. If he returns, I'll put the story out that he's trying to get me to pay him money to go away. You've already shown that a few fabrications in a good cause are excusable."

"Actually, I already made up a reason for Cleese's behavior." She felt embarrassed to admit how easily lies came to mind, but they had to make sure any stories they circulated agreed. "I had to say something when Toby announced to the entire household what the two of you were discussing. So I told them the stranger must have been deranged by the war. A few of the returning soldiers who have stopped here have been decidedly odd, so my reason was believable."

Joshua somehow turned her in the cocoon of his coat and placed a soft kiss on her forehead. "You are indeed my brilliant wife. A man might fabricate an imaginary child in the stress of battle and then come looking for him."

"I'm not sure my story will hold up to close examination." She leaned back so she could look Joshua in the face.

"But it was a good place to start. If we have to, we can add the blackmail threat to the excuse you've already established. Someone who's unstable might think of that angle as well." His hands smoothed the sides of her head, pushing her hair back. He looked deeply into her eyes. "Would you have shot him?"

She'd been expecting this uncomfortable question. Only the truth would suffice, even if she weren't sure what the truth was. "I hope I'd have done so if it were the only way to protect Quin. But I wouldn't have wanted to. The dueling pistol is part of a pair I found in the house while you were gone, and Mr. Daniels taught me how to use them. A few years ago, a pack of wild dogs was worrying the sheep, and Daniels was concerned that I might be attacked." She gave him a deprecating smile. "It never happened, but I suspect I would have shot in the air to chase them away. I didn't want to shoot a wild dog and am even less sure I could have shot a man."

His hands rubbed her temples in a mesmerizing rhythm. She felt herself relax into his stroke. "I would have sworn you had no qualms," he said softly. "I've never seen anyone so fierce. I've long suspected I was in error in thinking of you as my little brown wren. Today, it all became clear. In the place of that unassuming bird, I saw a kestrel. You have all the right attributes. They're the smallest of the falcons. Compact, brown, possessing an uncanny ability to ride the wind before swooping down on some unsuspecting prey, kestrels are fierce defenders of their nests and hunting areas. As you stood there, holding that pistol with such assurance, I definitely saw a kestrel."

Like the bird he'd just described, he swooped down and captured her lips. Arms that had earlier lightly encircled now pulled her tightly against him. He kissed her with an almost frightening ferocity, the hard ridge of his need pressing into her. He lifted his head suddenly. "When I realized you'd overheard what we were talking about, I was afraid you'd hate me," he said. "I put you through so much, and then…Quin might not even be my child."

She shook her head in an effort to deny his concerns. "It doesn't make any difference. Quin's ours to raise. He's long been the child of my heart." She didn't add that a few sweaty minutes didn't make any man a father. A father was a man who gave a child love and care, a man who kept his promise, even if he had to ride out on a bitterly cold day to find a pony. In these, as well as a myriad of little things, Joshua was proving to be Quin's father. Diana needed no other standards to know this was true.

She could tell Joshua was hurting over what had happened. Major Cleese's revelations had exposed Joshua's relationship with Quin's mother as a complete fantasy. The ongoing nature of the woman's betrayal must cut him deeply and make him question his relationship with all women.

She suddenly feared that the tender shoots of a loving life together, which they'd been nurturing for these past few months, were being threatened. "You're a good man, Josh," she said. "I've known that for a long time."

Then she pulled his head back toward hers and kissed him with all the love she had in her heart. He responded with a desperate passion, igniting a molten heat between them. Her feet left the ground as he cradled her to his chest and began striding toward the house. She gave a sharp shriek of surprise and then held tightly to his neck.

"We need to reassure the staff," she said.

He hugged her more firmly and brought his lips next to her ear. "Later," he whispered, nibbling at her lobe. "We'll worry about that later. For now, I selfishly need you."

Most of the household staff were hovering near the side door when they entered. Joshua didn't stop. He simply said, "All will be well," and continued carrying her up the stairs. She ducked down into his chest, feeling embarrassed, but not wanting to stop before they reached his intended destination.

He let her slide to her feet when they entered his bedroom. He turned back and locked the door. Then he was behind her, his clever fingers working at her lacings. "Where did you hear about men measuring their cocks against each other's?" he asked, when her gown was loosened and floating toward the floor.

Oh, good heavens. She had made that accusation. "The shearers who come to Harkley once a year. They say all sorts of things to each other while they work and never take my presence into account."

"Hmm," he murmured against her nape, as he sent her corset and chemise to the floor as well. "Would you like to learn some other descriptions even your shearers haven't used?" His hands reached around her to fondle her naked breasts. "For instance, I could use soldiers' terms to describe what I'm doing to you now."

And then he did, the words crude but accurate. He slid his hands down her body to nestle between her thighs, as he continued his verbal tutorial. She was sure she'd heard some of the terms before, but had never imagined what they meant.

As he continued to stroke her body, she tried to turn in his grasp so she could face him, but he held her imprisoned with him at her back. She was hot and wet before he rolled her onto the bed and joined her there. He came over her in silence, as if no crude terms could describe what they would now do. Or perhaps there were no words in a soldier's vocabulary to accurately chronicle behavior that was more emotional than physical. She only knew that like all wise birds, she flew.

CHAPTER NINE

THE BRIGHTNESS OF THE morning light sliced around the curtains and pulled Joshua from his sleep. Good Lord, how late had they slept? He reached for the pocket watch he'd left on the bedside table and squinted at the numbers. It was still early. How odd. The light was wrong.

He slipped from the bed and padded across the floor to the windows. Pulling the curtain to one side, he gazed out at a white world. It had snowed heavily overnight. Big, lazy flakes still drifted down to join the piles of those that had already fallen. It had certainly been cold enough for snow for the past few days, but this early into winter, he'd not anticipated it.

The white burden bent down the limbs of the trees in the park. The ground seemed to be mounded with feathers, and the roof of the distant stable appeared covered with meringue. It was a fairy world that called to his boyhood self to come out and play.

He looked back at the lump on the bed. He knew that under all the covers, Diana lay in boneless repose. His lips tipped up in a smile of male satisfaction. They'd used the bed for good purpose, both before dinner and after. She'd earned her rest.

But, like all young boys, Quin must be awake and anxious to answer the call of snow forts and snowball fights. He'd be disappointed that he couldn't ride Caprice. When Joshua had introduced Quin to the little mare last night, the boy had glowed brighter than the lanterns. After frolicking around in the snow, however, they could still work on basic horse care in the barn. Not as exciting as riding, but Quin would probably still find that activity enjoyable.

Joshua quietly moved to the dressing room and slipped into his warmest clothes, eagerness lending his movements haste. He gave one last look at the slumbering form on the bed. Tenderness for his strong, bright wife nearly overwhelmed him. He'd misread her all those years ago and was just now coming to realize what a treasure he'd been gifted with. Yes, she was a kestrel, and he needed to be willing to let her fly free. But he prayed he would prove worthy enough for her to always return to his glove.

He turned away before he succumbed to the urge to awaken her. He subdued his desire to kiss her sleeping face, to breathe in the scent of warm woman that was uniquely Diana, and quickly quit the room, taking the stairs to the nursery two at a time. His heart overflowed with love for both his wife and his child, for Quin would always fill that spot regardless of what anyone else might say. The day that lay before him beckoned with the potential for great happiness. First, a romp in the fresh snow with Quin, then breakfast, hopefully with Diana, followed by some time in the stables that might include all three of them.

Filled with anticipation, he pushed open the door, only to be met with silence. "Quin?" he called.

The boy's nurse came to one of the side doors, folded shirts held in her arms. "Good morning, Lord Trent. Master Quinten has gone to the stables to look at his new pony. I hope that's all right. I dressed him very warmly since I suspect he will end up playing in the snow if that scamp Toby is in the barn." She chuckled. "There's no keeping a boy in on a day like this."

"Thank you. I'll look for him there." Joshua gave the nurse a smile, but disappointment took the edge off his joy. Quin was already abroad, doing alone what Joshua had planned to do with him. Joshua felt cheated, since he'd wanted to share Quin's enjoyment. He mentally kicked himself. That last thought was a selfish one. And why would Quin even expect him to appear? After two months, they were still getting to know one another, and Quin had been providing his own fun for years. Joshua consoled himself with the knowledge that he and Quin could still spend the day together.

He detoured by the kitchen on his way to the stables and filched some cheese and rolls. Boys were always hungry and he'd not had breakfast himself. He exited the house to discover that the gardeners had already cleared the path to the stables, a good thing, since the snow would have come higher than Quin's knees and made for hard going.

As he followed the path, Joshua listened for the shouts of a snow battle going on. Since he heard nothing, he assumed Quin was still in the barn. When he entered and called the boy's name, however, the only reaction was that both Not and Caprice poked their heads from their stalls.

"Quin," he called again, wondering if he'd missed him outside. Only Not's chuffing sound of greeting broke the silence. Then he heard a groan, soft but distinct. The sound immediately drew him to a vacant stall. One of the grooms sat slumped against the wall, making incoherent sounds. He'd been tied up with long harness reins and a gag was stuffed into his mouth. Next to him lay a boy-sized bundle of clothes.

"Oh, dear God." Joshua's blood froze and he felt light-headed. Dropping the bundle of food he'd been carrying, he leaped into the stall, squatted next to the boy, and rolled him over. It was Toby. Relief flooded him, followed closely by concern. After a quick check for wounds, he placed a hand on Toby's chest and felt it rise and fall in a regular rhythm. Beneath, the boy's heart beat strongly. Some of the tension leached from him. Toby was unconscious, but didn't seem to be grievously hurt.

He turned his attention to the incapacitated groom. Jerking the cloth from the man's mouth, he growled, "What in the hell happened?" as he began working on the man's bindings.

"That man you warned us about came and took our Quin," the groom said, his distress bringing out an Irish brogue that Joshua hadn't previously noticed.

"How long ago?"

The groom paused to consider, tears in his eyes. "Maybe half an hour."

Joshua cursed under his breath. Cleese had a good head start. But the snow would slow him and make tracking easy.

"It's my fault. I heard the boys in the stable, but I was finishing up the repairs on these ribbons," he jerked against his bonds, "and I figured it was just the boys, larking around with the new pony, you know. But when I walked out of the tack room, someone hit me over the head and I woke up here. Is our Toby...?"

"Probably hit on the head as well." The last of the bindings parted, and Joshua sat back on his heels. "I'll take Toby up to the house and see if we can get the doctor to come on such a day. Are you in shape to saddle Not?"

"Yes, milord." The man got clumsily to his feet. He leaned against the wall drunkenly, giving the lie to his condition, but Joshua decided he could function.

"If the doctor gets here, have him check you out as well," Joshua said, going over to lift Toby into his arms. The boy's eyes blinked open and then slowly closed again. A good sign? He had no idea.

"Your lady does some doctoring," the groom said.

Joshua nodded. Of course she would. Diana had more knowledge and talent than the ordinary woman. But if Quin were lost, it would break her heart. "Use the heavy saddle I brought back from the Peninsula." He was going to war and needed to be equipped for it.

As he carried Toby down the shoveled path, he felt his old pre-engagement calm settle over him. Sounds were sharper. Everything he saw was crisply outlined. His heartbeat slowed and his muscles moved smoothly. This ability had brought him safely home, and he would see that Quin came safely home as well.

***

Diana hummed under her breath as she walked down the stairs toward the dining room. She should be worried that the early snowfall had caught the shepherds by surprise and they hadn't gathered the sheep into the folds, but all she could see was the magical beauty of the transformed landscape. She had confidence that any problems with the sheep would sort themselves out. She refused to allow concern to dampen her buoyant mood.

In the midst of yesterday's troubles, she felt that she and Joshua had reached some sort of accord. Together, they could manage any threat to Quin. They were a united front. She smiled as she remembered Joshua's tender lovemaking from the previous night. United was definitely the operative word.

Her grin was still in place when she reached the foyer and heard raised voices and loud footsteps coming up the stairs from the lower floor. She was surprised when Joshua swept into view carrying—good Lord, was that Quin?

"It's Toby," Joshua said, answering her unasked question. "He's hurt."

"Parlor," she said, joining the small train of kitchen staff that followed in Joshua's wake.

"I think he's been hit on the head and is unconscious," he said, laying the boy on the settee. "His breathing and heartbeat seem normal."

She pushed by a gawking scullery maid to kneel next to the settee. She realized other members of the staff filled the door. "Other than Cook and Putnam, the rest of you, out."

She ignored the general milling about, her attention focused on Toby. Joshua's assessment was correct. She gently ran her hands over the boy's head and found a large lump behind his left ear. When she touched the spot, Toby moaned and tried to brush her hand away. Hopefully, this signaled a return to consciousness. Toby was the son of one of the laundresses and a stableman husband who had not taken to marriage and long ago disappeared. But he was a good boy, always helpful. "I need snow wrapped in a towel and some warm blankets," she said, confident her instructions would be followed.

Someone touched her shoulder and she looked up into Joshua's concerned face. "I think he'll be okay," she said.

The look of fear didn't leave his face. "Cleese has taken Quin." An incoherent cry leaped from her mouth and she started to stand. He kept pressure on her shoulder. "I have to get some things upstairs and then I'm going after them. I'll see you before I leave."

She wanted to ask him more, but he had already turned and was striding out of the room, pulling

Putnam along behind him. She heard the two men talking in the hall, but by then, Cook had come back with the cloth-wrapped snow. Her focus returned to the supine boy.

Toby's eyes were open and he was talking by the time Joshua again entered the parlor. He carried saddlebags, a holstered pistol, and a carbine in a saddle scabbard. She immediately stood and went to him. He enclosed her in his encumbered arms and she felt some of the tension flow out of her.

"I'll bring him back," he murmured. "I know you love him. I'd walk through fire to give you your heart's desire, so I don't think snow and ice will stop me."

She pushed back to look up at him. His green eyes were dark, but looked more intent than worried. "I know you'll bring Quin home."

He started to pull away, but she held fast to his coat. "Be sure you also bring yourself back unharmed," she said. "As much as I love Quin, it is you who's my heart's desire."

A look of joy flashed across his features. He gave her a quick kiss, and then he was gone. She could do nothing but turn back to the boy who needed her help and pray that the two most important people in her life would soon be restored to her.

CHAPTER TEN

THE DEEP SNOW MADE the tracks easy to follow. But the travel itself wasn't easy. Even following the other horse's trail, Not had to plow his way through chest-high drifts. It made for very slow going. Joshua was so cold he hurt. He hated to imagine his horse's discomfort, but Not kept up his ground-eating walk without complaint.

He had no doubt that he would get Quin back. Regardless of what Amanda had written, he doubted she could be certain of the boy's paternity, especially if she were sleeping with both him and Cleese. Intellectually, the major had to know the same thing, and he certainly couldn't have any emotional attachment to Quin at this point. Joshua's hope was that he could buy the man off. He'd filled the saddlebags with every bit of cash in the estate safe. He was sure Diana would agree this was the best use for the money.

And if Cleese wouldn't take the bribe and disappear—well, Joshua was also well armed. He just didn't want to use that option.

Joshua was relieved to see that the stride of Cleese's horse had shortened. The animal must be tiring. He had no idea how far behind he was, but with Cleese slowing, he'd catch up all the faster. He just hoped it didn't take too many more hours. He hated the thought of trying to return to Harkley in the dark. Except for the areas where the road was bordered by hedges, it was difficult to ascertain exactly where the thoroughfare was. As he followed the tracks, he noticed Cleese often lost the direction.

He became even more concerned when Cleese turned off the main road onto a lane. The snow-covered bushes along the verge had evidently convinced Cleese he'd chosen the best route, but Joshua knew the lane only led to a derelict farm. He doubted that was the major's intended destination.

When the hedgerows disappeared, the trail left by the previous horse and rider wandered erratically until it finally cut cross-country. Couldn't the idiot tell he was traveling over uneven terrain and going downhill? As Joshua followed, worry gathered into a solid lump in his gut. Cleese was heading toward Mickleson's Pond.

It had been cold enough for ice to form, but this particular pond was spring fed, and the churning waters seldom froze completely. Even a thin layer of ice could support the snow, however, making Mickleson's Pond invisible. Dread as frigid as the wind gripped Joshua, and he urged the laboring Not to greater speed.

When he reached the top of a low hill, his fears were confirmed. The area where the pond was located was a smooth expanse of white. It looked like an easily traversed, snow-covered meadow. And that was what must have lured Cleese into crossing it.

His eyes followed the tracks onto the pond's surface, tracks that ended in a gaping hole. Joshua's heart stuttered to a halt. "No." The word came from his mouth as a low moan, like the sound of wind in the eaves. It could not be. It couldn't end here.

As if he felt Joshua's urgency, the big gray horse began leaping through the drifts. As he drew closer, Joshua saw a dark, still shape to one side of the ragged hole. Too small to be a man. His breathing stilled. Yes, it could be Quin. Dear Lord, let it be Quin.

He stopped Not and dismounted. He carefully walked forward, testing the ground under him with every step, the horse following behind. When Joshua's footing indicated he was on ice, he pushed on Not's chest, backing him until the big animal appeared to stand on solid ground. He dropped the reins to the ground and hoped the horse would remember his training and act as if he were tied.

Joshua then gingerly stepped out onto the snow-covered ice, moving toward the pile of clothing he hoped was Quin. The body looked so damned far away. He tried calling the boy's name and thought he saw movement, but he couldn't be sure. It might have been hope and the uncertain light. He took one step and then the next, waiting for the ice to crack beneath him and pull him down into the dark waters.

Finally, he felt the ice sift under his feet. He was close, so damned close. Slowly going down onto his hands and knees, he lowered himself to his belly, trying to distribute his weight over the largest area possible. He began to swim through the snow, moving his arms and legs like a frog. His progress was slow, but it was progress. The snow piled around his face, smothering him and burning as if it were fire.

After what seemed like miles, one questing hand made contact with some material. Joshua forced his stiff fingers to close. Once he felt he had a firm grasp, he began to swim in reverse, trying to stay in the compacted area he'd already made. Quin, he was sure it was Quin, lay unmoving, but slid along in his wake. Pain sliced through him, an agony worse than when the French bullet had pierced his side. What if he could only return to Diana the dead body of this beloved child?

He renewed his efforts. Quin couldn't be dead. Joshua hadn't come so far, both today and over the last few years of his life, for this quest to end in defeat. He crawled backward for an eternity. And then his feet hit a solid object—Not's massive legs, rising from the snow like frozen trees. He'd made it to solid ground.

He painfully stumbled to his feet, pulling Quin into his arms. "Live, live," he chanted over and over. The child was so cold, so still, but he thought he felt him breathe. He rubbed his hands back and forth over the small body, trying to create warmth with friction. A corner of his mind registered that Quin's nurse had indeed dressed him warmly, but was it enough?

Joshua opened his greatcoat, now stiff with crusted snow, and the hacking jacket beneath. Then he stripped off Quin's heavy outerwear and placed the boy next to his own exertion-heated body. Quin felt like a shard of ice nestled under his heart. Joshua folded his coats around the child, remembering he had done the same thing with Diana. Was it just the night before? It seemed like a hundred years ago.

Quin moved against his chest. He moved! It was not his imagination.

Joshua awkwardly mounted and set Not back on the track that they'd made. He pushed the tired animal into a trot and then a bouncing canter. The light was going, but their path was obvious. He knew, nonetheless, that the big horse was making a heroic effort.

Quin squirmed against him, the pressure filling him with joy. A small, gloved hand made its way out the neck of his coat, followed by a face pressed into the opening. "Uncle Josh?"

Joshua's eyes filled with tears and he dashed them away before they had the opportunity to freeze on his lashes. "Yes," he said, "it's Uncle Josh. I'm taking you home."

"The man stole me. And then, when his horse bounced, he threw me away," Quin said.

"He was saving you, so I could come and take you home."

"Oh," Quin muttered, and then he snuggled down within the coat.

Joshua realized that what he'd said was the truth. Cleese may have stolen Quin, but at the last minute, when he realized his error, when he saw the lethal waters coming up toward him, he'd tried to throw Quin to safety. And now it was up to Joshua to get Quin all the way home.

***

The doctor didn't arrive until nearly dinnertime, but he did come, having to abandon his gig in favor of a long, cold horseback ride. Diana was thankful he'd made the effort. He checked Toby over and found him on the mend, although he recommended the boy spend the next few days in bed to make sure there were no aftereffects from the blow to his head.

Diana offered the doctor dinner and a bed for the night, both of which he quickly accepted. He pronounced the night as one safe for neither man nor beast, not realizing how his words cut Diana's heart. All through dinner, she only toyed with her food, her entire attention focused on listening for a horse arriving.

When Joshua hadn't returned by dark, she mentioned to Putnam that they should put out some lanterns to guide Joshua, and hopefully Quin, back home. The staff had outdone themselves. The entire drive, from the gateposts to the house, was now lined with blazing torches. Members of the staff tromped through the cold, patrolling the area to make sure that none of them sputtered out. The torches made a brilliant arc, an arrow straight into the heart of Harkley.

And still, Joshua did not come.

Diana went to her bedroom and undressed, if for no other reason than to let her maid find her own bed. But Diana had no illusions about going to sleep. She paced the room but always returned to haunt the window that looked toward the front of the house. Her breath fogged the pane, turning the torches into a trail of solid light. She told herself that Joshua might have wisely stopped for the night at an inn, but deep in her heart, she knew this was not the case. If he'd made it to the village, he would have come on to Harkley. The next closest posting inn was too distant to be of use in this weather.

The fear in her was a living thing that upset her stomach and left her close to tears. What if something had happened? What if he were lost in the snow, or that madman had killed him? During all the war years, she'd known he might not return, but this was very different. The man she awaited was different. If Joshua hadn't come home from the Peninsula, she would have gone on. Now, she wasn't sure that would be possible.

The tears finally breached her defenses and rolled down her face in silent drops, but she would not give up her post at the window. Joshua would come. He had to.

And then she saw movement near the end of the lane. She frantically wiped her eyes and rubbed the frosted glass in an effort to clear her vision. Yes, it was a big horse, head down, walking with a stumbling step. On its back, a man sat, hunched forward as if clinging to the pommel to stay astride. A man without a boy. Joy and pain warred within. One of the torch tenders must have called an alert. Men came running from the house and the barn.

Regretting that she'd changed into her nightclothes, Diana grabbed a shawl and ran into the hall as she wrapped it around her. Her feet flew down the stairs and toward the front door where Putnam hovered. As she went to brush by the butler, he put his hands on her shoulders to stop her, very un-Putnam-like behavior. "Stay here, my lady. They're bringing them in."

Them? Them! She pushed forward and saw one of the grooms carrying a small bundle while two others followed, walking on either side of Joshua, offering him support. The tension of the last hours broke and tears streamed down her face. "Build up the fire in the parlor and rouse the doctor." Then she went running out into the frigid night, only to stop on the porch. The most important thing was to get both Quin and Joshua into a warm room and to pour hot liquids into them. She reversed her direction and dashed to the parlor, throwing instructions in her wake.

Quin arrived first, carried in the arms of a long-legged groom. He looked at her with sleepy eyes, like any child his age awakened from a sound sleep. Relief coursed through her. "Uncle Josh saved me," he said.

"Yes, I know he did." She looked at the groom. "Put him in the big chair near the fire." She kept any other instruction until later, since Joshua was being helped through the door.

She rushed to him, reveling in the feel of his arms closing around her. Ice crystals covering his coat bit into her, but being held was worth it. "Thank you. Thank you," she muttered into his cold chest.

The doctor arrived, his nightshirt stuffed crookedly into his breeches and his hair askew, but he was alert and ready to take charge. He issued orders faster than a general and had the entire staff running. The entire staff? Diana looked around and they were all there, dressed and ready to work. It seemed that no one at Harkley had slept this night.

She relinquished Joshua to the doctor's care, but when the man suggested she retire, she told him she would not be excluded. She must have done so emphatically, since it drew a chuckle from Joshua. It was the first sound he'd made and was as welcome as rain on parched land.

Muttering dire predictions of possible lung fever and definite frostbite, the doctor went to work. After what had to be hours of applying warm compresses, he proclaimed his patients out of danger but in need of sleep. Quin had already taken his advice and snored softly in a wingback chair, a thumb having found its way to his mouth as it had when he was much younger.

Diana saw Quin installed in the nursery and then returned to the parlor where only Joshua remained. He held a glass of brandy in gauze-wrapped hands. His chapped face was shiny with an ointment that filled the room with the fragrance of chamomile. He contemplated the fire with tired eyes.

"Come to bed," she said, careful to touch him only on the arm. His hands, feet, and face were all painful.

"In a minute. No one asked what happened, and I hope they never do, but I wanted you to know."

His voice was raspy, and she was about to tell him this could be handled in the morning, but his intent stare told her whatever he had to say was important to him now, not at some later time. "Thank you. I would like to know." She took the chair recently vacated by Quin and faced him.

"Cleese is dead." She must have given a start, because he answered an unspoken question. "No, I didn't kill him. He inadvertently tried to cross Mickleson's Pond. It was covered with snow. There was no way he could have known…" He paused, gathering himself for what she knew was coming. "He and his horse fell through the ice. But before that happened, he threw Quin clear."

He took a sip of his brandy and looked back into the fire. "I've been trying to puzzle that out all the way back. It kept me somewhat alert when I was so cold and tired I just wanted to fall into a snowdrift and sleep. But I couldn't do that to Quin." He chuckled softly. "Hell, I couldn't do that to Not, who I guess I'll forever have to call Lover's Knot, since the beast has earned a fancy name." His attempt at a smile was weak, but beautiful to Diana nonetheless.

"I spent a long time trying to figure out what went through Cleese's mind, both in taking Quin and in his actions at the end. I'll never know for sure, of course, but I think he loved Amanda. Knowing what she was, knowing all of her faults, he still loved her. I suspect he didn't know who Quin's father was any more than I do, but that didn't make any difference to him. He saw Quin as part of Amanda, and he had to have him. And then, at the end, when he realized what was happening, he didn't try to save himself. He saved Quin—because he'd unconditionally loved a flawed woman and wanted part of her to live on."

Joshua turned from the fire to look her in the face. His eyes were the deep green of spring grass in the shade, and needy. Oh, so needy. "And I wondered all the way back if you, knowing all my faults, could ever feel that way about me."

She moved without thought, going down on her knees, lying across his lap to hug him around the waist. "Oh, my darling, I'd forgiven you long ago. You don't have to earn my love. You always had it—and you always will."

"Thank God," he said in a choked voice. "I love you so."

Then his bandaged hands pulled her up his body to kiss her, and she knew they were both home.

EPILOGUE

Spring, 1815

"Don't go so fast," Diana yelled. She knew Quin had heard her, since he gave her a cheeky grin as he and Toby thundered by, dashing toward some imaginary finish line for their race.

"I'm talking to the wind," she said with resignation.

Joshua chuckled, the low sound reverberating from his chest and into her back where she leaned against him. "Oh, Quin hears you. They both do. But the male of the species is incapable of following external instructions when engaged in competition.

That's one of the reasons I'm hoping your cute, little bump turns out to be a girl." As if to emphasize his comment, Joshua loving trailed his hands over what was decidedly a bump.

Once she'd told him she was expecting, Joshua had been fascinated with the process. Heavens, at night, he'd kiss her distended tummy and talk to the child within. Of course, she'd yet to arrive at the truly ponderous stage. Diana hoped he still found a walking barn appealing, since that was the direction she seemed to be heading.

"I thought you wanted a son," she said. "You've always said we were on an heir hunt."

He nuzzled her neck and whispered into her ear, "Why do you think I'm hoping for a girl? Or even three girls in a row. That way we have to keep hunting and hunting."

She laughed and turned in his arms. He looked relaxed and happy as he slouched against the trunk of a chestnut tree, the glowing clusters of the white flowers hovering high above his head. Her happiness would be complete except for the shadow of another war with Napoleon. The former emperor had escaped from Elba and arrived in Paris to a hero's welcome. England would have to fight him once again. Joshua had followed the call to battle before, and she could not be sure he would not do so again. The uncertainty ate at her.

"You do know that Quin asked me how the baby got out," he said with a smile.

"Heavens. What did you say?"

His grin widened. "The same way the lambs get out of the sheep, of course. And I'm very happy he hasn't been around when the rams are servicing the ewes, or he might have a somewhat skewed idea of how the baby got there."

He laughed aloud at the look of horror that evidently flashed across her face. "Diana, children will wonder about these things. I bet you did."

"I asked such things when I was much older, and then I was given the tale about finding babies in the garden." She was surprised at how prim she sounded. But, *like sheep*? If she'd been told that at six, she'd have had nightmares for weeks. The lambing season was just a few months past, and Quin had helped care for the orphans, but she'd had no idea he'd been there when some of the ewes had given birth. They'd have to keep a closer watch, or Quin would discover how babies ended up in their mother's stomachs. Or at least one method. She felt color rise in her cheeks. The thought was truly embarrassing.

Joshua might be right in hoping for a girl. Diana was sure females had to be easier to raise. At least, in her experience, girls didn't ask impertinent questions or go thundering around on horseback. As if conjured by her thoughts, the boys came whooping back, racing in the other direction as they leaned over the necks of their ponies like jockeys.

"There are times I question the wisdom of getting Toby a pony, too," she commented dryly. "Quin would much rather ride with him than with either of us." Of course, she'd just begun to ride when she'd told Joshua of her condition. He'd immediately suggested that she stay with both feet on the ground for the duration of her pregnancy. Since she'd still felt uncomfortable and wiggly and awfully far from the ground, this had seemed like a good idea.

"Toby more than earned that pony." Joshua brushed away a chestnut blossom that had drifted down to land in her hair. "When I discovered he'd actually tried to get Quin away from Cleese—" His face took on the slightly haunted expression that appeared when he thought of that horrible day. "It's a good thing for Quin to have a slightly older friend. To have someone at his back."

"I was just considering that we now have four potential broken legs instead of two." When Joshua laughed again, she joined him. Her life overflowed with joy. And she wanted it to stay that way. Unable to avoid the topic that bothered her, she asked, "You're not going to put yourself in harm's way again, are you? I know troops are gathering in Brussels…"

Joshua slowly shook his head. "I'm not going. I've had my war. I've done my part. I think I've earned some tranquility. I owe you and Harkley all my attention, and this is where I'll stay. I love you, I love this land, and I love the bump. I want to be nowhere else."

"Thank heavens," she said, threading her arms around his waist and pulling him close. His hand traced down her back as he nestled her into his body. He smelled of growing things and promise. She'd never imagined a moment of such perfect happiness. But contrary to all her earlier expectations, she'd found it, and she wasn't going to let it go.

AUTHOR'S NOTES

I've always been fascinated by the repercussions youthful mistakes have on later life—so much so that this has inadvertently become a theme in many of my tales. Today, such lapses in judgment can be recorded on a cell phone and immediately posted on YouTube for all to see. I'm relieved that such devices weren't available during my own age of stupidity, and this attitude probably helps keep my characters firmly rooted in the pre-technological past.

I hope you enjoyed Joshua and Diana's story. If you have any questions or comments, please use the comment form on my website – www.hannahmeredith.com. or visit www.facebook.com/HannahMeredithAuthor. I love to hear from readers.

Thanks,
Hannah

ACKNOWLEDGEMENTS

By its very nature, writing is a solitary business, but no book appears out of a vacuum. I've had a tremendous amount of help and encouragement along the way. If I were to list all the seminars, classes, organizations, and individuals that have helped me in my endeavors, the list would be impossibly long—so most will remain unnamed. Those who had a direct effect on my present writing are, in alphabetical order, since sometimes a friendly ear is needed as much as a critique: Anna, Barbara, Carolyn, Cathy, Kate, Marie, and Marion. Thanks to you ladies for everything. The whole gang at HCRW has also been incredibly supportive. I so appreciate your collective wisdom. And most importantly, there's Bob, without whom, everything I do would be meaningless.

Made in the USA
Coppell, TX
11 July 2022

79805268R10066